Colourful Characters *of the* Older Ireland

Tom Neary

Greann Publications

DEDICATION

To my wife, Carmel and our family – Ann, Michael, Pauline and Thomas.
To their spouses – Tony, Margaret, Tom and Gillian.
To my grandchildren – Sarah, Rachael, Hannah, Kate, Emma, David and Anthony.

First Edition: 2021

British Library Cataloguing in Publication Data
Neary, Tom
Colourful Characters of the Older Ireland

ISBN no.: 978-1-5272-8904-8

Images by: Shutterstock, iStockPhoto, Alamy, Wikipedia, Private Collection. Other images have been attributed to the source where possible. Apologies for any that may have been inadvertently omitted.

Layout & Design: Sinéad Mallee
Printed by: IngramSpark

CONTENTS

AUTHOR'S NOTE

In this Collection of Stories, which is a mixture of fictional and non-fictional offerings, please note that all the Characters and Places mentioned in the former ones are entirely fictitious. Any resemblance to present-day individuals and places is purely coincidental.

The same is true of the Characters in the non-fictional pieces but in them, the Places are real.

The Aim of this book is to entertain and at times, to inform. It is meant to be a FUN BOOK and is not written to ridicule or criticise anybody.

It was born as a result of the Coronavirus epidemic when people had extra time to both read and write. Many were asking for something light to cheer them up and to relieve the boredom.

The Seanchaí on Mickey Joe Gooseberry

An occasion that was looked forward to was the visit to Cosy Kitty's Bar of the Seanchaí– the traditional storyteller. He called around, now and again. I made a point of being present on one occasion. As soon as he arrived, Kitty planked a fine pint of Guinness in front of him and the show began.

He said there was a man, in his father's time called Mickey Joe Gooseberry and he became very busy, spreading the news that he was on the lookout for a wife. He left no stone unturned in his search for the ideal lady of the manor. He was no spring chicken, well over the fifty-five mark, but he had a definite preference for a woman in her twenties. When Gabby the Gawk heard of his advertising, she felt nauseated and said that he must not have awoken from his daft dreams.

Mickey Joe lived in a very pretty village known as Thonemore and he had the locals driven mad there with his soft romantic chat. The man of wisdom there, Paddy Scar Face, met Mickey Joe one morning and sat him down on a low fence for a chat. He told him bluntly that there were no suitable or eligible girls in the area at all, and that he would have to go farther afield.

Mickey Joe listened carefully to his advice and then asked Scar Face what would he suggest. He thought for a moment and then said: *There is a small town not too far away, you know it well. It is called Poteenbeg. Jack the Knack has a pony and trap and he would drive you there. You may know that the town is noted for two things, mineral waters, not the lemonade kind but waters that are good for your health, like sulphur, iron, phosphate and more. You may not be too interested in the springs or spa, but the other thing about the town is that it has many matchmakers and they meet people in the pubs. Many women, looking for men go to the pubs and many of them are introduced to what may become their husbands. They are also good drinkers of the waters as they are health conscious.*

Mickey Joe agreed to do the pilgrimage to the place of prospect and Jack the Knack was called in to do the trip.

He was told to reward him financially for his time and trouble and drinks should also be included. The deal was done and off they went on one of Jack's Tours.

Scar Face told Mickey to seek out Crab McDonnell, that he was the best matchmaker in town. He was into a great deal of soft chat, being kind of handy with the tongue. Mickey did as he was told and met the said matrimonial expert. Crab began by saying to him that choosing a wife is not the same as going into a shoe shop and asking for a particular size, colour and quality of shoe. It is far more complicated than that and not all demands may be met in any one individual.

With that Crab introduced him to the first of three women present in the pub. She was Daisy very small, petite, if you like. She had red hair and a very cold frosty face. Mickey eyed her up and moved away a little and said to Crab that red hair scares him. He thought that there was too little of her in it and her face resembled an eminent snowstorm. He told Crab to move on to the next woman.

She was Cheryl, much more substantial than Daisy. She had a big round face resembling a full moon in Autumn. She had a tanned face and a big tattoo on the side of her leg. Mickey asked what it was and she said that it was the Garden of Eden, with Adam and Eve. He was overcome completely with that. When she spoke she was very noisy and Mickey said that you would think that there was a hurricane on the way. He had enough of this and asked Crab to move on to number three.

The third woman up was Gloria. She was of average height and size and reasonably good-looking. Her voice was soft and pleasant and she had a nice smile. She was stylish, too, and was a good chatter with a great laugh and sense of humour. Mickey was impressed and told Crab that he was pleased with her and would he arrange for them to meet again. Gloria was interested and they would meet again the following weekend.

Jack the Knack was employed again to do the transport bit and he had many months of it, to the point where he was getting tired of the trips. Eventually, things came to a head and the wedding date was announced, but it was known only to a very few people. It took place in Poteenbėg Church of the Martyrs on April Fools' Day.

All unnecessary frills were eliminated and the Reception was earthy. The menu was simplicity itself – bacon , cabbage and spuds in their jackets followed by jelly and custard and if one felt like a drink, there was plenty of water from the well and good buttermilk.

When the meal was over the newly-weds made their way over to the pony and trap accompanied by Jack but when they got there, the pony was missing. Jack, at once, contacted the local Garda Station. The Guards said that they would investigate. They then got a man with a horse and sidecar to drive all three home.

On the way, there were bonfires burning for the couple but unfortunately, at one of them an old man had tripped and fallen into the fire at Lugnalack crossroads. He was taken to Drakeford Hospital. As a result, the newly-weds were upset.

The following day, Jack got good news. The Guards found his pony grazing in a field, two miles away from the church.

They did not bother at all with a Wedding Cake but when they got back home to Thonemore they enjoyed a porter cake that Mickey had made himself and from their home base, the honeymoon was spent walking in the neighbouring hills, for a few days.

When the locals got to know Gloria they loved her as she turned out to be a very kind, generous and sociable woman. As time went on, the couple reared five children and then they went their separate ways. The eldest lad, Marco became a professional comedian. People enjoyed his story about the folk he knew that loved the environment so much that they could not leave it. One guy made a bed for himself on top of a big oak tree and slept in it every night and was thrilled with the birds' dawn chorus in the morning. The kids enjoyed this and used to pass by the tree at night singing *"Sparrow in the Treetop".*

Another fellow built a hut on top of Ben Dubh mountain and only left it to get some food and water. He used to sing his own songs including *"She'll be coming round the mountain when she comes".* It is not the same way they all go and it is just as well.

A third one, this time a lady, occupied a big cave on the coast and lived in it all the time, on fish and seaweed.

The fourth in the family was Petula and she was an excellent singer. She joined a band as lead vocalist and did well for herself, driving around in her Mercedes. She married Slack Jack from Pollagorra North. He was an acrobat.

The youngest family member became a magician of note and he travelled widely. He was able to make things disappear and pull rabbits out of his pockets. He used to cut up people in two halves and put them back together again. He used to swallow fire and play with snakes. The children adored him and he used to give them false faces, lollipops and balloons.

As the Seanchaí's story came to an end, the audience gave him a clap and Kitty gave a free drink to all present.

Mickey and Gloria are still alive and well but their transporter Jack the Knack died two months ago. Crab is still plying his trade and thriving on it as he gets a nice fistful of notes for his trouble every time he has a successful introduction.

Johnny Fiddlesticks and the Twins

I met a neighbour of mine recently and he asked me did I ever meet Johnny Fiddlesticks Fogarty who lives over in the village of Brambletown. I replied that I had not and then he advised me to go and have a chat with him, that he loves recalling olden times and much much more.

When the weather improved I decided to make a trip to Brambletown on my rather quaint bicycle as the journey was only a few miles. I made enquiries as to where Johnny Fioddlesticks lived. There is a long steep hill leading up to his abode, so I had to walk up the hill with my bicycle.

Johnny lives in a small thatched whitewashed cottage, very neat and tidy, as was its surroundings. He has a nice name-plate on view outside. It reads *"THE PALACE".* I knocked on the door and the response was prompt from inside. The Lord of the Manor appeared, in living colour. Greetings were exchanged and then we both sat down on a nice comfortable bench outside the cottage, for a chat.

Johnny is not a very tall man but what gets your attention is the way he dresses. He wears a baggy trousers which is a deep green colour. His shirt is a bright red and it is partly hidden behind a multi-coloured, ornate waistcoat. His jacket is a brilliant white and a big orange-coloured scarf hangs down loosely over the jacket. You could easily mistake him for the national flag. The shoes are a royal purple and do not fit in well with the rest of the attire. His grey beard adds distinction to his big round face.

As it was Autumn he began telling me about harvesting, in days gone by.

He remembered the golden fields of ripe oats and the shivering fields of barley. They were so beautiful to look at, with the wind shaking the ears of corn like the waves on the ocean.

The crops were harvested with scythes and one could hear the sound of scythe stones, sharpening the blades of the scythes, resembling a symphony orchestra.

Prior to the scythe, there was only a sickle or reaping hook and one can only imagine how slow and tedious the work of reaping must have been then.

When a swath of oats or barley was mown with the scythe it had to be taken out and made into sheaves. Each sheaf had to be tied with a straw rope and then thrown out of the way of the next swath. This process went on all day, until the job was finished.

The sheaves had then to be put standing up in stooks, six or eight sheaves, in two lines. The stooks had then to be tied with a straw rope as well. At the end of a day's work, the stooks in a field, in neat straight lines, looked like soldiers in battle array.

The stooks were left in the fields for some time, to season before they were transported into the haggard and there, put into big stacks or reeks which had to be thatched with straw or rushes, as protection from the weather. Sometimes, the sheaves were simply put into a shed. If the crops were left out in the fields, stacks had to be made of them there and thatching was necessary.

The women helped out in the harvest fields with the men as many hands made light work.

Fiddlesticks then moved on to another aspect of work. He began talking about the day set aside for the threshing of the corn. When a thresher came to a village, every farmhouse in the village that had corn was looked after, on the day or on the following day.

This was a *Meitheal* occasion when all the farmers in the village came to help in the work with their forks and they moved from house to house until all the threshing was completed.

Some of the men stood on the stacks and forked the sheaves up to the men on the roof of the thresher and they fed the sheaves into the machine through an opening on the roof.

Other men, hung canvass bags on hooks, at the side of the machine to catch the corn as it dropped down the chutes into the bags. When the bags were full, they had to be removed and empty bags attached.

The threshed straw emerged from the machine at the front and fell down on the ground. Men then removed the straw and made a big long reek of it in the haggard or put it into a shed. The chaff would be left on the ground but farmers often used it for bedding in the barns and stables.

The machine was powered by a tractor which was connected to it by long heavy rotating belts.

Earlier on, there were horse powered threshers when all the work was manual and earlier still, all people had were flails which consisted of two strong poles of wood, tied together. The longer of the two was held in the hand and then the sheaves of corn were threshed with the shorter piece. The wind was utilised for winnowing or taking the chaff out of the grain.

During the threshing operation there was usually some drama and excitement because numerous rats and more particularly, mice could be seen scurrying, all over the place with cats and dogs chasing them. It was the warmth of the stacks of corn that attracted them.

The threshing occasion was a time for work but it was also a social occasion. The villagers all came together and after the work was done, at each farmstead, if there was a woman in the house, she put up a fine meal for the men and there might even be a bottle of something stronger than just tea.

There are still some threshers to be found in Ireland but times have changed and so has work on the small farms. Many farmers, especially in the

West do not grow cereal crops at all, preferring grassland for grazing.

On the big farms in other parts of the country, the combine-harvester is now the in-thing. It combines three operations at the same time, namely, reaping, threshing and winnowing, which is very handy indeed.

Combine-harvesters would not be feasible on small farms because of the cost of them and the lack of reasonable acreage.

I then asked Johnny had he any brothers or sisters. He replied that he had two sisters. When they were going to primary school the kids gave them nicknames and they stuck with them for life. They christened them Hurdy and Gurdy, very likely because they were twins.

When they grew up, they emigrated to California and got work in Beverly Hills. Now, they were not involved in the film business in Hollywood, so they never won Oscars but they were involved in the fashion and beauty business and rubbed shoulders with the greats of the Screen. They supplied them with expensive outfits and hair styles. About a year before my visit to Johnny, they came home for a visit to the green and misty island, as they put it.

Johnny could not believe how they had changed. They were the essence of style, gorgeous fur coats, fabulous hats laden with feathers and flowers, dazzling jewellery, sparkling like the stars of the firmament. The whiff of their perfume would suffocate you and the ear –rings were more like the wheels of a cart. He felt out of his depth, to be sure.

It was clear that they were filthy rich but they failed to enrich his kitty. They did give him a gift, however. It was a framed picture of Mickey Mouse and Minnie herself, direct from Disneyland and bearing their signatures.

Hurdy and Gurdy stayed with Johnny for three days and he was glad to see the back of them, but one thing they were keen on was Irish music, so Johnny, being a brilliant violinist, hence his nickname, Fiddlesticks, enthralled them with his wonderful selection of jigs, reels, hornpipes and more. They told him afterwards that he put on a jolly good show. After all, it was free and it cost them nothing.

The day before they left, the local Gossip, Tina Turkeycock Timlin met them on the road and delayed them greatly. She gave them a thorough questioning and asked them were they married. The answer was "No". Like Fiddlesticks himself they lived in single blessedness or whatever you want to call it.

Tina did not hand out any Oscar to the pair either but she did comment later and gave her verdict quite publicly – *They might have been the cream, but someone forgot to make the churning. Were they to remain on in Brambletown for any length of time, there would soon be many empty houses and the emigration figures would show an increase. It is a blessing that their bags are packed for lift-off.*

As soon as life got back to normal and the twosome had left the Emerald Isle, the local atmospher became relaxed again and Johnny's blood pressure got back to its proper level. Then he took the framed picture of Mickey and Minnie and threw it into the fire. He told me himself that he did not bother collecting the ashes.

Johnny said to me that he heard a smart man say that when a person or persons visit a place, their presence remains there after them. He believes that now, strongly, because he said, ever since Hurdy and Gurdy departed, the strong pong of their perfume pervades the entire residence. What a legacy! What a legacy indeed!

Daffodil Delaney over in Poll na Muc had a similar experience. She said that ever since Aunt Sarah visited her, the smell of her is all over the house and ventilation does not shift it. She has not said what kind of a smell it is but her friend Bushy Head is certain that it is not perfume.

I thanked Johnny for his time and his reflections and bade farewell to Brambletown as the evening sun was sinking on the western horizon.

It is indeed amazing the variety of human beings that one encounters or hears about some of which are lovable, charming and entertaining and others who might do nothing to lift the spirits. However, the mixture ensures that our world is less boring, for you know that variety is the spice of life.

The Rambling House in Cloonleamh

I heard a good deal of talk about a place called Cloonleamh and my attention was drawn to it, so I travelled there in order to see what goings-on take place there.

One very fancy cottage caught my eye and I asked a man walking with his bicycle who lives there. He said that an elderly couple were the residents there for a long time, Barney Bumblebee Brady and his wife, Corncrake. Then he said *Have you never heard of this house?* In my ignorance I said - that I had not. *Well,* he said - *That is the rambling house or if you prefer, the visiting house where the neighbours gather in every night to chat and play cards.*

I thanked the man and then went as far as Barney's cottage, knocked on the door and he opened up. I asked him could I join the neighbours that night as I would like to play cards and meet the people. He willingly agreed and I was very pleased that he was so agreeable and friendly.

That evening I arrived in good time so as not to miss anything. Corncrake herself was handing out cups of tea and scones to everyone. She was a very tall woman and she towered over me and others who flocked in for the night. She was chatty, pleasant and welcoming.

During the refreshment period, all interesting local happenings were well thrashed out and opinions expressed, some in favour and others not.

A topic of interest was the General Election to be held the following week. The local candidate, Eddie Joe Blackthorn was present and he was full of soft chat and pressing hands wholesale. The locals say that his soft chat is all that is soft about him.

He approached me with his hand stretched out and said that he would be speaking in public, outside the church in Cloonleamh on the following day. He actually invited me to hear his speech. He gave me a leaflet about himself and his policies.

Barney then called the gathering to attention and asked them to sit around the big kitchen table for the card-playing session. The first part of it would be a poker session.

It was generally believed that Barney would win, every time, as he has done for many years now. When he plays he dominates everyone and intimidates them to a point where they are afraid of him. His personality changes from being a saint to being a tyrant.

True to form, he cheats every time, keeps the cards to himself and if anyone asks to see his cards, he explodes and goes into a tantrum. All is then silence. The reason for his act is to make sure that at the end of the night he has a good pocket full of money, so the household gets back anything that may have been spent on the tea and scones. There is no such thing as a free lunch. At the end of the session he blessed himself and said - *Thanks be to God! I had a great night's work.*

The second session consisted of games of Twenty Five with teams of two people playing together. It is not a session for beginners because most of those present are seasoned players and they get very annoyed when the less experienced players make mistakes and destroy the action. I was lucky in that my partner was an excellent player, a guy called Silver Tongue Cassidy.

That is exactly what happened on the night. It was serious because the same night the prize for the winners was five hundred pounds, big stakes indeed. A young lad, Billy Pat Dick was in partnership with Badger Robinson.

Badger was usually very awkward and he began to fight with the lad because of playing the wrong card. The rest of the players tried to break up the scrap but that drove Badger farther. He drew out and plastered the young fellow with his big hand.

Fair play to Barney, he grabbed Badger and sat him down. That brought the altercation to an end but it upset all present. In case I forget, Barney and his partner, Gullet Looney claimed the prize as was expected.

In times past, card-playing was a man's world but in more recent times women have joined in and even youngsters which balances the budget.

Just as the men were about to leave Barney and Corncrake's house, a Guard knocked on the door and said that Wrinkles Milligan's Baby Ford had gone off the road and into a dyke over in Mangebeg as the road was icy. He said that Wrinkles was not injured or perturbed. He was sitting in his seat singing "Rafferty's Motor Car".

The Guard concluded that there must be more than an icy road that caused the accident. His opinion was that he could have had a gallon of stout in the petrol tank, as the song says.

He asked the men to join him, to see if they could tow the stranded vehicle and its occupant on to terra firma. They all agreed to help and in a short time, Wrinkles was retrieved. The car was not damaged as it only hit soft material. Wrinkles wasn't sure was all of this real or was he just dreaming.

I took a B&B in the Chestnut Tree Hotel in Cloonleamh so that I would be near the Church there to hear the bold Eddie Joe speak on the following morning.

After the midday Mass, His Lordship appeared on the back of a truck and began his oration. What follows is an edited version of his words.

My dear electors, greetings!

As you know I have been chosen to be your Independent candidate in the forthcoming General Election. It is a great privilege to be representing such a progressive, intelligent and hard- working people as you are. Congratulations!

You know well that I have served you well in the local Council for a long time and now I am moving up a notch to do even more. I know your needs, inside out and you know that you can always trust Eddie Joe to deliver the goods.

A fellow in the crowd shouted up - *I must be blind because I could never see anything you did and as regards delivering the goods, the truck must have broken down somewhere on route here.*

I will now spell out for ye what I intend to do for you, the proud people of this area. Footpaths will be put in, on all approaches to the village. Street lighting will be installed. New gullies to take the water off the roads will be put in place. Road signs will be displayed in all necessary locations.

Transport will be provided for the elderly so that they can get to places of their choice. Jobs will be created for all classes of people, from the skilled to the unskilled and play areas will be provided for the children.

As you know, politicians in the past have made all kinds of promises but they have not delivered, in any shape or form. I am not like them. I deliver.

People have come to me about the vast wilderness of rocks and stones that ruin down to the shore of Lochmore, that great big scenic area of water at your doorsteps. Well, believe you me, I will see to it that every rock and every stone there will be hurtled into the lake, never to surface again and all the land will then be reclaimed and beautified.

I could go on and on but I know that you know that I need not go into too much detail. I know that you are happy to leave everything in my capable and willing hands. You can always trust Eddie Joe.

There were many interruptions and hecklers. A well-dressed lady in the crowd shouted *Can we bottle the hot air?* another remarked *When did you return from Disneyland?*

Eddie Joe's parting shot was - *Make sure you give me your No.1 when voting. In that way you can insure your future. You can always trust Eddie Joe.*

I heard today that Badger Robinson regretted his quarrel with Billy Pat Dick. He has apologised and has given him a present of a newly born suck calf.

Barney and Corncrake will be travelling to the Bahamas in a fortnight's time as they have won the prize in a big Raffle held locally. Money seems to follow Barney in particular.

A few days afterwards I heard that Wrinkles Milligan was in trouble again going home from Larry's Lounge. The road turned and he didn't and the Baby Ford went straight into Johnny Blister's pond beside the road and stood upright in a few feet of water. Wrinkles seated inside, let down the car window shouting for help. Luckily, a local garage owner spotted the car and towed it out with a tractor.

Wrinkles said that he thought that the steering must have malfunctioned but the garage man did not agree. He was a witty man and he gave the proper diagnosis. The mishap was due to misjudgement resulting from over-indulgence of an alcoholic substance.

As of now, it seems that Wrinkles is good to go, once more but one gets the feeling that his chances of continuing survival may be running out.

When the election votes were counted Eddie Joe missed the cut, did very poorly and lost his deposit. Another local politician of a different mind-set, topped the poll.

As I was walking down the street I met Gerry Noodleman and he began talking about the election and politicians. He was of the opinion that the politicians in the past were better than they are today, good speakers, anxious to achieve and serve well, the people who elected them. They had less soft chat, were honourable and straight with people.

There is no doubt but that politics always interested Irish people, down the years. This may be due to some extent to the country's history of strife and struggle. Sadly, only men became involved, apart from the few towering women who were brave enough to get dug in, in order to achieve the aims in which they believed.

It is encouraging today, to see more and more women running as candidates for elections and being elected to serve in Government. Perhaps, this trend will continue into the future and lead to a better gender balance in Dáil Éireann.

The New Residents of Ballyhuha

Farming today is a very important industry and the modern farmer is very skilled and well-informed. He or she loves the land and cares for it because it is essential for making a living and rearing a family.

Those who have grown up on a farm have a great advantage over those who have no knowledge of farming at all, but who often take up farming, in the belief that all that is necessary is just to go out and buy a piece of land. This approach does not always work out well.

It is not hard to find an example of this. Down in the village of Ballyhuha North is a couple, who some time ago, returned from Birmingham in England and purchased a small farm with a cottage there. They had no knowledge of farming at all. Neither of them grew up on a farm and while in England, both of them worked for a long time in a circus.

The neighbours took a great interest in the new arrivals and they seemed pleased with them and welcomed them. Nevertheless, they kept a close eye on their activities.

The first thing requiring attention, according to Hugo was the pathway leading to the cottage. It needed a good coat of gravel, so he read an Advert in the local paper, advertising a tractor and trailer for sale. He contacted the seller and made the purchase.They were fairly old items and Hugo did not examine them closely like an experienced farmer would, before parting with money.

Hugo set off without delay to the quarry to get a load of gravel but he had gone just a mile of the road when the tractor cut out. It was good for Hugo that he was not far from the local garage, so he walked over to the mechanic there and told him his story. His name was John the Bulldog and he rescued Hugo as he got the tractor up and running again.

Hugo reached the quarry and the bossman there gave him a big heaped up load of nice gravel, not too rough and not too fine. He sat up and drove the banger home. When he pulled up outside his cottage, his wife, Elsie came out and said: *Hugo, what are you doing with the empty trailer?*

In utter amazement, Hugo viewed the empty trailer. Was there some magic at work? Then he spotted the reason for the empty trailer. It seems that the floor of the blessed thing must have been rotten and gave way under the weight of the load. At least, the three miles of road between the quarry and the cottage got a nice bit of gritting, helpful in frosty weather.

Elsie emerged from the cottage, solemnly, like the Pope coming out to give his *Urbi et Orbi* blessing. She almost went on fire when she realised the true nature of what happened. She had no notion of giving any kind of blessing, as it turned out.

She instructed Hugo to detach the trailer from the tractor, at once, and then she sat up on the tractor and drove it out to a spot overlooking the hill in front of the cottage. Whatever way she left it, it got wander lust and moved off down the slope to the bottom, hit a big bush and then burst into flames as did the bush. A neighbour looking on, who happened to be Pimples Duddy, said that he was expecting Moses to appear at any moment, but he failed to show up.

When the owner of the quarry heard of Hugo's misfortune, he delivered a free load of gravel to his cottage and a neighbouring man, Eddie Jim Pat gave him an old tractor that he had done up himself, in order to help out.

Hugo then turned his attention to acquiring some livestock. One morning, a truck pulled up outside the cottage and a rough looking guy shouted to him, to get his attention: *I heard you want to buy some cattle. Well, I have three good beasts here in the truck.* Hugo jumped at the opportunity. He was looking for three heifers so that they would have calves, eventually and milk for their tea and coffee. The deal was made and the animals were releases into the nearest field. They looked fine and they at once grazed away.

A few days later, Pete Frosty Face passed the way and met Elsie who was boasting about the fine heifers her man bought and nothing would do but for him to see the purchases. With that, he hopped over the ditch, and eyed them up. *Elsie,* he muttered: *They are three fine bullocks ye have there, but ye will not be having any calves or milk from them.*

With that, she dashed back into her kitchen, grabbed a bottle of whiskey and downed it, raw. Shortly after, she was talking to herself and searching for Hugo who was not to be seen. He was in the local pub, the Swaying Tankard, practising relaxation techniques. Just as well, because the alternative would have been an Elsie tongue – lashing.

Elsie decided that she would carry out the next livestock purchase. She wanted to buy some sheep so that they would have lambs and wool for sale, in due course. She saw an Advert in the local paper, offering six sheep, at a discount price. At once, she jumped to it, contacted the seller and he duly arrived with them in a trailer. She counted them and the six were there, right enough. The seller, Mophead Greensleeeves opened the trailer and put them into Elsie's field. They seemed to enjoy the good grass.

A week later, a neighbour by the name of Ginger Jack passed the road and saw the sheep. Being a smart farmer himself, he took an interest in the animals. He spoke to Elsie who was out in her front garden. She told him of her purchase and how they would be having lambs and wool, in no time at all. Ginger paused, and said to her, with a long face - *I'm afraid ye will not be having lambs or wool at any time because what you have there in the field are all rams.* With that, Elsie changed colour, but I am not in a position to record her finale here, as I have some respect for the reader.

When Hugo came on campus, Elsie related the sheep story to him and he was anything but pleased that another foofaw had occurred. He did not attack her, however. She got away with a nasty look. After all, neither he nor she, covered themselves in glory, so far, in the world of farming. Hugo said: *I think we are in the wrong business.*

The following day, Ginger called in to the pair of them and said that he had a small gift or two for them. They could not believe what they were hearing. He brought them a young cow, a heifer and three ewe lambs and to really put the icing on the cake, he gave them an adult ewe as well. He said that they were surplus to his requirements. They were bowled over with his kindness and generosity.

By degrees, the sun began to shine for them a little. A week later, another local man, Fancy Pants Mulligan who was a carpenter, called and put a new floor in the trailer, for free. There is no doubt but that the people who lived in Ballyhuha were decent, generous and had a good community spirit.

The neighbours had been so kind and generous to Hugo and Elsie that they decided to do something themselves in order to return people's goodness to them, in some small way.

They contacted the village spokesperson for the local community. She was Mary Josephine Cauliflower, talkative, in the extreme, colourful, exotic and suntanned, but it was not a Ballyhuha tan, of course. The locals called her Thunderbolt and you could certainly hear her, long before she would come into focus.

The couple put her the question: *"What could we do that the local people would like"*? The answer came quickly, loud and clear. She said that as they had years of experience in a circus in England, they should put on a show for the locals, and especially for the children. They thought that was a great suggestion, so they set to work to do just that.

In no time at all, they put their show together and advertised it in the local newspaper. It would take place in the village playground, outdoors and would be free for all. The news went down extremely well with everyone. The day passed and soon the big evening arrived. A crowd filled the playground very early and some local women served snacks and tasty bites. The atmosphere was electric. A great show followed the introduction by Mary Josephine Cauliflower.

The show opened with a big dance number performed by Elsie, elegant in her sparkling dance outfit, while Hugo blasted out the rhythm on his big trumpet.

Then he sang numerous songs and the crowd joined in. Next, the pair did some acrobatics and juggling, throwing lighted torches up in the air and catching them on the way down. They even had dogs jumping through hoops.

Hugo acted the circus clown and did four of his favourite clowns – Do Do, So So, Go Go and Mo Mo. The kids loved all four presentations and clapped and cheered loudly. Sweets were thrown to the kids also, so everyone enjoyed the evening.

It ended with Hugo walking through the village on very high stilts which for many, was the highlight of the show. Everyone returned home happy and grateful to the circus couple, now turned farmers.

I nearly forgot to tell you that the couple have attended two major farming Courses of late, so now they are able to hold their own with the very best of the local farmers and gone are the days of the stupid mistakes that nearly destroyed them. As is said often – all is well, that ends well, and so say all of us.

A very striking thing about rural Irish people, the majority of which are and were farmers, is the great closeness they always had and still have with one another.

When and if one is in trouble or in need, the neighbours rally around to help and support. In the past, in particular, this joint effort was referred to as the Meitheal, a Gaelic word meaning a working party.

This custom reflects true Christianity in action, loving the neighbour as yourself.

Vortex McQuillan-Meteorologist

Have you ever heard tell of Vortex McQuillan? For the locals, he is just Vorty. Now, Vorty is something special, even unique, some would say. Years ago, he qualified as a meteorologist, and although he never got himself a job, he believes that there is nothing that he does not know about the weather.

He lives down in a small village called Wetland and even the village name is a reminder of climatic activity. The land around it is certainly marshy and soggy, so when traversing it, it is recommended that Wellington boots be employed. Smelly Billy, over in Crankstown described it as snipe land, and he is not far off the mark.

Whenever you happen to bump into the said Vorty, it will not be long until he launches into the topic of weather, and especially the current meteorological situation. At once, he will confound you with weather terminology, highs, lows, fronts, depressions, occlusions, and top of the range is a Vortex. When he mentions that, the situation is very serious, so you had better prepare for the worst. You will then have a great excuse to go for a pub crawl.

Should you attempt to cut in on his flow of speech, he gathers speed and cuts you out of the conversation.

Penelope Goodweather from Madamore has summed him up superbly. She says that some natural disaster such as a hurricane or tornado will blow him into oblivion, because he is a pain in the ankle in the morning, at midday and especially in the evening, when he has fully revved up. The worse thing about him is that he keeps repeating himself, like a needle that gets stuck during the playing of an LP.

In order to have scope for his weather lore, he widens his area of transmission. He dallies in the small local grocery shop, run by Biddy Smalltop who came to Wetland from Scunthorp in England. Prior to that she lived in London, where she developed a Cockney accent. She is now more Irish than the Irish themselves, but she cannot stand Vorty at all. She has composed a Litany of her own, for him, and it is not the Litany of the Saints.

Another favourite location is over at Maggot Brady's farm where her meets up with several farmers who are always interested in the weather situation. He was over there, some time ago, and he did so much talking that hoarseness set in and his voice eventually packed up. The Maggot gave him some over the counter medication and as it was a very warm sunny day, Vorty lay down by a fence and fell asleep. The sky darkened and the sun disappeared before a massive thunderstorm struck the area and it was followed by a prolonged downpour.

On waking up, Vorty became aware that he had been totally and efficiently baptised with water, if not by the Holy Spirit. All of this misfortune, however, was just a temporary interruption, so Vorty just played on, to everybody's annoyance.

When Vorty was in his thirties, he went for a short break to Blackpool in England. While there, he met a redhaired lady by the name of Imelda Potterton. On his return to Wetland he kept corresponding with her and after a period of seven years, they tied the knot.

Coming to a place like Wetland, for a posh urban lady like Imelda, was a shock to her system. She had been a trumpet player in an English band, but now she could play her own trumpet for Vorty, in her state of matrimonial blessedness.

Vorty's favourite song, and he was no Boccelli, was *Singing in the Rain,* for most of the year but at Christmas it was always *Let it Snow, let it Snow, let it Snow.* Imelda was a good singer and dancer, so the locals, as they are wont to do, christened her "Twinkletoes", a nickname that she never grumbled about as she was an easy-going type. In due course, she formed a small band and even taught His Lordship a few tunes which he enjoyed while on a break from weather forecasting.

The couple lived in an old world bungalow with an apple orchard at the front and at the rear of the residence was a small pond which contained edible fish. They used to go out a few times a week fishing, in their small boat. Imelda used to cook the fish for dinner and it was no harm to let her cook, for she was very skilled when it came to cuisine.

A special hobby that they had was rearing and breeding goats and they usually had about fifteen or sometimes twenty of them, in a large plot of ground bordering on Shady Shauna's premises, of poor repair. Goat's milk and especially Goat's cheese were in big demand in the locality, so Imelda used to sell both items in Biddy Smalltop's little store.

As regards the neighbours, they kept out of Vorty's way, as much as possible, owing to his weather mania, but Twinkletoes was not a problem as she was reserved, quiet and pleasant. She kept to herself and troubled nobody. As a woman, she was very good-looking, tall and attractive, far too good for mo dhuine.

As Mike the Mawler put it: *She's a deluxe model.* Whiskers McGinty put it another way: *I believe that she would sit better in a palatial mansion in Beverly Hills.*

Vorty himself is some very unusual bit of architecture, to be sure. When good looks were being handed out, he must be out of town. His face is like the highs and lows of the Connemara mountains, a face that has suffered much severe erosion. His hair resembles an overgrown meadow in the depths of Summer. To be honest, one could expect to find an element of wildlife therein.

He walks with a slant to the right from the perpendicular, resembling a leaning tower. As Julia the Cricket Moriarty remarked: *"I wonder has he Comprehensive, because if he falls over, he could injure someone for life and could be sued for thousands".*

Winking Willie added that the man would not have the cop on to insure himself, and anyway, his meanness would stall him up, so it would.

Recently, Vorty had a brainwave. He decided to build a weather station at the back of his bungalow, to prove his dedication and devotion to the elements. Without delay, he got going, with the help of some paid labour who, under his instructions, erected a small prefab hut. In the fullness of time, the project became a reality.

The neighbours were amused and thought that the man had dropped down to zero, in his head. They looked at the structure and just passed on, without comment.

When the Station was fully fitted out, the bold Vorty announced on local radio that Wetland would henceforth have a state of the art weather service.

In the Wetland area, there were two real boyos who were the architects of many great pranks there, when opportunities arose. They were Kinky Kelly and Dinosaur Peacock. They should have Degrees for their devilment.

One evening, they knew that the couple had been invited to the opening of an extension to the local pub, the Stumble Inn. While they were away, the two boys arrived at their residence with a truck and a JCB. In no time at all they had loaded up the prefab and all its equipment and set off with it, on a journey of twenty miles, until they reached an old derelict castle in the village of Foggytown East.

They drove up a hill where there was a perfect view of the countryside and relocated the Weather Station there, an ideal spot for such a project. The boyos said that there would not be any official opening ceremony, then or later. With that, they all adjourned to Crazy Eddie's bar, in another village called Scruffybeg.

In the brightness of the following morning, all was revealed. Vorty and herself thought that they were in the wrong house, as the view to the rear was different. Then, suddenly, they noticed that the famous Weather Station was gone.

Thoughts floated around in their heads. Did the wind knock it down or blow it away? Did the fairies take it or some leprechaun? Maybe someone was practising magic or illusions? Could it have been stolen by some gangsters? The questions rolled on.

Whatever transpired while they were away, they did not know. One thing is certain, however. The Wetland natives will have a bit of a wait for their next weather bulletin.

When the Hump Murphy heard about the great disappearance, he drew out the moral of the story. Said he, with a slight grin and winking his bad eye: *It is fine to be smart but sometimes it is a bad thing to be too smart as you can get under people's skins, and that's it.*

The latest breaking news is that a FOR SALE sign has just gone up, outside Vorty's homestead and Guards were seen there, some time ago. It appears that they traced the Weather Station and informed the couple of their findings. They made their way to Foggstown East and have purchased a new bungalow there beside the old castle, from which they can see their Weather Station, on the hill.. The owner of the bungalow, Bartley Cyclone, is leaving permanently, as he is involved in research projects in the Arctic circle, including the North Pole, so Santa Claus will have a new neighbour. Wonders never cease!

One of the most common topics of conversation in Ireland always was the weather, maybe because we get so much bad rainy conditions with a very limited amount of sunshine. Of course, the weather is a very safe subject and it is good for a chat when nothing else comes to mind.

In the past weather forecasting was quite basic and some fellows set themselves up as weather experts, giving long-range predictions and many believed them. Today, with all the advanced technology and trained meteorologists, forecasting the weather is very accurate and science- based. This is very necessary now in view of global warming and for alerting the public about approaching hazards.

Fruitcake McAdoo and Son

Fruitcake lives in a small thatched cottage in the long sprawling village of Ballinahoo West. Her real name is Dolly. Her nickname derives from the fact that she makes great fruitcakes and sells them down in the local shop, run by spritely Smokey Sally. She lives on her own as her husband alias Dan Michael Ned McAdoo died some years ago from over indulgence in the black stuff and potent spirits. His nickname was Rhubarb as he grew a garden full of it.

Those who were acquainted with him, always had a good helping of poteen, which for those not in the know, we are talking about the real native Irish brand of spirits, illegal, of course.

He learned how to make the blessed drink, strangely enough, in Scotland where he used to go every year picking potatoes. The Scots called the stuff Red Biddy, and if you refuelled on it, you would see stars and much more.

Dan Michael Ned was a great man to tell stories or yarns, if you prefer the word. But you could not believe one word that came out of his mouth. He never, ever told it as it was, unlike his smiling wife, Fruitcake, who always told it as it was. He used to spread all kinds of rumours and often scared people out of their skins.

One example of this is the one he told down in Crooked Face's pub. He said that the Pope had landed down from the sky in a very big balloon and that

Pakey the Gawk had driven him to the Church in Gortnahone, in his ass and cart as he wanted to speak to a black sheep, a big sinner in the village, known to the dogs in the street as Hilda Harriet Hornby.

He was indeed a pleasant and jolly man and there is no doubt but that he must have caused some disturbance in the heavenly realm by now and a bit of laughter.

As to Dan Michael Ned's general appearance, we will leave that to Eileen Cauliflower Finnerty. She said that he was well-proportioned, well-dressed and well fed but that he walked with a stoop in him as if his face was trying to make contact with his big toes. She called this phenomenon completing the circle.

Coming to herself, she is the remains of a good-looking woman who had her ups and downs in life, on her small farm. However, she survived. She is of medium height and build, with an oval-shaped face and big eyes, resembling traffic lights. As Warty Slattery remarked and he is an expert on human anatomy – *The lady can be described as regular, in every respect, apart from her turned out feet, one bearing North North West and the other, North North East, as if they are not on terms with one another.*

She reared a son, popularly known as Scollops, because while he was around home, he used to sell scollops to the locals for thatching houses. He was not much of a lover of the small farm as he thought that he could not make a living on it, so he packed his bag and emigrated to England. He got work there in a fancy hotel in Birmingham, which suited him well, as he would not dirty his hands, too much.

His mother was very good at letter-writing and the day I was in her village I paid her a visit and as it happened, she was sitting at her table in the kitchen and was just after writing her letter to his nibs.

Without further delay, she handed me the letter and said that if I wanted the latest news circulating in the locality, I had it all there. I thanked her and asked her how her son was getting on in England. *Mightily well,* she replied.

The following is a copy of her letter –

My dearest darling Scollops,

I know that you love to hear all the news from home as it keeps you in touch with your roots. I was glad to hear that you are happy in Birmingham town. Ye probably have a bit more traffic on the roads there than we have here in Ballinahoo West.

We often had more news but it seems that the cold weather has made the locals hibernate. I can tell you however, that the Rabbit Doherty fell out of his standing on Monday night in Cringer's butcher shop and died on the spot.

He was never any addition to the human race. As Mary Ann Bisto remarked: The world will never miss him. There will be less bad air. He generated too much hot air in his day.

Scribbler the postman got beaten up down in the townland of Splutterbeg. He had a row with Clout Drury and he is a very awkward bit of goods, if his feathers are ruffled. The postman had opened his mouth too wide and said more than he should. When Roddy the Frog heard about the altercation, he said that a closed mouth catches no flies.

The Brady quads are home from Philadelphia. They are four fine women now. It is a pity that you could not meet one of them, marry and settle down. Maybe you could come home and I would use my skill in coaxing one of them to walk out with you.

The Drake sisters are completely cut off in their residence and cannot get out. Flood –water has engulfed the place. Alphonsus the Shark has a small boat and he is to have them evacuated tomorrow. In the meantime, they can have a good wash, so they will be immaculate when they hit dry land. It's a question of water, water, everywhere.

I must tell you about Weasel Waters. He spent last Friday night up in the Happy Bar and as he is emptying the pint glasses very fast, at present, he is in no fit condition to be at large at all. Close to midnight, His Lordship emerged from the bar on to the main road.

He grabbed his less than de luxe bicycle and when he got to the middle of the road, he attempted mounting the machine.

In a shot, the bicycle spun around on the very icy road and down he came, in living colour, on top of the banger. It was well that no car happened to come along. There he was, looking up at the starry sky and singing "The Fields of Athenry" – Low lie the fields...

To be sure, he bore a resemblance to them, for he was low-lying, as low-lying as one can be, now stretched out flat on an icy road.

The Digger J.D.Duffy came along and pulled him in to the side of the road. He loaded him up on his old Baby Ford, bike and all and left him home. He would live to see another day, just about.

Last week we had more drama here. Furnace Fogarty paid his weekly visit to the butcher, Aido Kidney and bought his usual few pounds of mutton chops. The butcher wrapped them up in brown paper and Furnace made his way out to his bicycle and put the meat on his back carrier, well secured.

Then, in a moment of weakness, he went up to Cranky Cissie's pub for a little liquid refreshment. He dallied there a while to hear all the latest scandal.

On his return to the parked up bicycle, he noticed bits of brown paper flying around in the wind. Then he noticed that the parcel of mutton was gone.

Nearby a big dog was happy-looking and still eating a piece of a chop. The dog enjoyed his dinner that day but it could have been Lent as far as Furnace's dinner was concerned.

We have got a new priest in the village, of late. His name is Fr. Marco Dando. All his sermons are about the next world. He said that he has given up on this one, because it has given God a very hard time. He said that he would not like to be God as the stress of it all would kill him.

One other addendum, regarding Scratcher Blackberry. He is now gone totally in the head. He thinks that he is Einstein one day and the next day the Ayatollah. He stands up on a wooden box in the village and gives a speech every day about the state of the planet, that is, Planet Earth. He wants to start a Revolution but he is not sure what his cause is or what his aim is. He always begins with the song – 'What a Wonderful World' – his own version, of course, followed by 'Forty Shades of Green'. He ends with either 'Amazing Grace' or 'Here I Am Lord'.

A voice from the assembled crowd shouted, jokingly, – Why don't you sing 'Paddy McGinty's Goat' or 'The Last Rose of Summer'? The man is bound to be locked up for good, shortly. Another less polite guy shouted up – Why don't you put a sock in it? Shut up your big mouth.

As my pencil is on its last legs, I will bring this epistle to an end. I will rush you more news as it becomes available.

P.S. If you have any spare notes, please bring them with you when you are coming back. We will find a hole for them.

Lots of love for now.

Dolly.

Your sweet evergreen mother.

I heard recently that Scollops came home from Birmingham to see if the mother could pull some stroke with one of the Quads. Philo had no interest in Scollops, neither had Jenny. Margo was undecided and Patsy said that she might test the temperature and see if there would be any chemistry between them, but nothing guaranteed.

Scollops is prepared to give things a try. Dolly is very pleased with this and maybe, in due course, all will end well and they can live happily ever after.

A concluding thought about letter-writing. It was a great activity in the years gone by, in the days before all the modern communication gadgets and the practices of texting and Emailing. They have killed off the art of letter-writing, in a big way. Now, there is no need for notepaper, pen, biro, ink, envelope or stamp and no need to head off to a letter box or post office to post the script. This is all very handy and it is almost instant linkage with the person or persons receiving the messages.

Laughing Larry and the Fairy Tree

One of the nicest places I have visited recently is the village of Rosetown. It is idyllic, scenic and pleasing to the eye. It lies in a long green valley, through which a very clean river flows.

Forested areas can be seen in the distance. There is an air of neatness and grooming all around. If it is a healthy environment that you seek, this place was made for you.

The village consists of about a dozen small well-thatched and whitewashed houses, all with smoking chimneys. In the very centre is the real gem, the tiny cottage of the Lord Mayor of the place, so called by the locals. He is none other than Laughing Larry Looney, so nicknamed because of his outstanding humour, tall tales and many adventures. It must be agreed that he has a very warm, pleasant and funny appearance. He resents the stiff upper lip type of individuals.

Gooseberry McGuire put it well when she said *Larry always reminds me of the rising sun, on the eastern horizon, early in the morning, or if you prefer, at the dawning of the day.*

Larry's homestead is worth inspection, on the inside. When you enter, the first thing you notice is a big open fire with plenty of black stone-turf creating a wonderful glow. The heat would remind you of a mini-hell or a minor inferno.

You must not miss the huge open dresser laden with beautiful willow pattern dinner plates and more, big fancy jugs, chinaware, large bowls, tea pots and tea canisters. You think that the woman of the house must be doing her job well, until you find out that she does not exist because Larry is a bachelor.

He never married because he said that the cottage dimensions were never meant for more than one individual. If a woman were to join Larry, she would not be able to turn left or right in this doll's house. At any rate, he is happy as he is, in the state of blessed singleness. He runs what he calls an independent republic and it is tax free.

Another highlight of the cottage is the ceiling of the kitchen. It is a mixture of things - large fletches of bacon, wrapped up in newspaper hang from the woodwork because Larry kills a pig every year to ensure a meat supply.

Large bunches of onions tied with cord also hang there because the resident likes fried onions and onion soup which he dispenses with flair.

In fact, he is quite a good cook. He makes lovely wholemeal cakes and is an expert with eggs and porridge. He does not have a cooker but he is well able to burn the daylights out of everything with his open fire on the hearth.

To the left of the open fire is a small bedroom, not the usual kind of bedroom. It is just a space for a bed which he refers to as the Hag. It has a nice draping of floral curtain at the front as you look at it. It is cosy, warm and comfortable and that is where Larry enjoys his slumber deep.

Step outside the cottage now because I must show you his lovely garden, brimming with great vegetables and as clean as a well shaven barber, not a sign of a weed anywhere. The prime section of it has beautiful heads of cabbage and what a great addition that is, to his bacon dishes for dinner.

The only thing that disturbs Larry's peace and quietness is when Raspberry Butterscotch calls to see does he need any help with anything.

He does not like her calling at all as she is overbearing, talks all the time, asked hundreds of questions all at once as if she is taking part in a marathon competition.

Her worst trait is that she uses awful bad language and she is as loud as a heavy drill boring through concrete. She would scare even the Pope in Rome. She could do with his blessing.

When the hurricane has passed, Larry recovers with the aid of whiskey, raw, always, never diluted with water.

Raspberry is now beyond picking but she has notions, of a sort, all the time. Rake Flaherty keeps an eye on her. He believes that she would move in with Larry if she could convert him to her way of thinking.

He knows Larry's mind, however, and says that the end of the world will come before that happens. It is a question of "Good night, shirt!"

Until last year there was a special tree in Larry's back garden. For ages past, the local people always referred to it as the Fairy Tree. Many tales have been associated with it. The local Seanchaí or storyteller would make the hair stand up on your head when he speaks of the Fairy Tree.

The local historian, Frosty Face Hannigan says that, one night as he was passing by the tree, it was all aglow with green lights. A Leprechaun was sitting on a big branch playing weird music on a violin and numerous elves were dancing around the tree, holding hands.

When Biddy Jam Jars heard the story she did not believe it. She concluded that the man must be three sheets in the wind after a night in the pub. After all, Frosty Face is a great fibber.

However, Frosty did not lay off. He coaxed Larry to allow him and the neighbours to excavate around and under the tree to see could they come on the crock of gold that fairies are supposed to have.

In due course, a Meitheal arrived equipped with spades, iron bars, shovels and such like and set to work. Larry sustained them with a jar of porter and sandwiches.

A progress report stated that the task was proving difficult as huge boulders were encountered around and underneath the tree. Despite this, the men pushed on and after some hours they had gone down yards into the earth.

I should tell you that the tree in question was an ancient oak, very high and spreading out, on all sides. The day itself was quite windy and like a flash of lightening, the tree broke loose from its roots and came crashing down, pinning two of the men under it and killed them, there and then.

The two departed were Knobs Murphy and Ale Can Clarke, both with a wife and a cart load of kids.

Work ceased and the push for gold was abandoned but Larry was determined to check out the last remaining boulder. He pushed it out of place with his iron bar and at once, a spring of water hit him in the face, knocking him over, but there was no crock of gold to be seen. The entire effort was like a swim against a waterfall.

The fallen tree is still lying on the ground where it fell and the excavated hole was never filled in. Larry has not gone next or near the site since. He is afraid to cut up the tree for firewood or touch the area.

The local women were not in favour of tampering with the Fairy Tree. Their spokeswoman, Biddy Jimmy Dick gave her verdict – *"The little people have powers of their own for self-protection because they do not trust people like us".*

Larry was lucky to have escaped the drama unscathed. It was good for him, too, that he had all of his property insured to cover the costs of the tragedy. They would be substantial.

The funerals of the two men who died at the excavation were very sad and hard on their families, relatives and friends.

The priest who officiated at the funerals was Fr. Billy Joe Wishbone and he said that, though we love adventure in order to get our longed for prize, there can be built-in dangers that we do not expect to encounter, during our quest. We never learn to consider that, which is a pity. It could make us cautious and a great deal more careful.

Those in attendance all agreed that the holy man spoke words of wisdom and perhaps many of them will keep his words in mind in future times and as a result, follow his advice and keep themselves safe from danger.

Funds for the bereaved are on the way.

Larry loves old things, especially old transport. His mode of travel is always in his antique Baby Ford, left to him by his grandfather. Now, it must be said that he has kept it in immaculate condition and everything in it works.

The kids love to see him careering down the road and blowing the horn loudly – the magnificent man, in his flying machine.

He is very careful with his precious vehicle and he always keeps it locked up at night, just in case some smart guys might cast an eye on it. He had one near shave, one night down in Tullybrack as he emerged from the Bumble Bee Lounge. That area has a bad name and some very undesirable specimens of humans have grown up there.

He was lucky to have come on a big gurrier about to break in to his Baby Ford. He had more luck when the Guards came along and arresterd the bucko.

A few miles away from Rosetown live two real boyos, always playing tricks on someone. They are Mophead Brady and supremo, Skillet Scully, in the village of Slimeybeg. They set their eyes on Larry and tracked his movements in his Baby Ford. He had a habit of going for a walk along the local river but to get to the place, he had to drive and then park.

While he was well away from the vehicle, in which he had left the key, the two devils stole the car and drove it to a village called Ballyknacker Lower where there was a very big hayshed, in a quiet isolated place, on a big farm. They drove the car into the hayshed and then covered the car over completely with hay, so that no one could see it. They left it there and took a shortcut home.

The following day the main news in Rosetown and farther away was the terrific fire that had broken out in Ballyknacker Lower. A hayshed had gone up in smoke and a car was burned out within it.

Larry, at once knew that the car must have been his Baby Ford but he was not certain of that. The guards did confirm that later. They said that it seemed to them that the car must have gone on fire, having overheated due to shortage of water in the cooling system. The guards are investigating and trying to track down the culprits.

Laughing Harry is depressed and is on foot presently, as he has no wheels under his anatomy. Larry has always been laughing, but now the laugh is on him. It was not a welcome prank carried out on a likeable man.

Raspberry called to console the victim and made a great speech. In fact it is still going on, as I write. I heard some time ago that Larry has equipped himself with Ear Plugs. Wise man, Larry!

Jumping Johnny on the Haunted Castle

I was talking to a friend recently and he asked me did I ever visit a place called Ganderville. I thought for a moment and said that I had heard of the place but that I had never visited it.

Then he said to me that I should visit it, that I would get a story there from a local storyteller. He tells it as it was, strictly factual and no fiction. It is a long way down there but it might be worth the trouble. He told me to find the house where Jumping Johnny lives.

I set out in my banger and surely enough it was a long drive before I saw any signpost for Ganderville. The roads were desperately narrow and winding and some were even covered with potholes. As I travelled along, the area seemed to get very remote, isolated and lonely. There were very few houses to be seen and it seemed to me that it would be very unlikely that one could get an evening newspaper there or any newspaper, for that matter. Suddenly, I saw a sign for Gurrier Castle, Ganderville.

—

I took a right turn and soon saw a mountain, quite high, in the distance. When I got closer I was able to see a great pile of old buildings that seemed to me to be derelict. I stopped and asked a man grazing cattle on the side of the road what the buildings were on the mountain. He said that I was looking at the ruins of an old castle, long abandoned and he told me that the village was farther on, up the road. I thanked him and drove on.

I stopped again when I saw a woman pushing a bicycle, laden down with bags and packages. I asked her did she know where Jumping Johnny lived. She said that I could not have asked a better person as she was his girlfriend. She said: *Swing to the left and then swing to the right, drive on a bit, swing again to the left, then to the right, on another bit and you are there.*

I was to look out for a thatched cottage with a deep blue colour on the walls and red windows and doors, the only one of its kind in Ganderville. I did all the swinging she told me to do and lo and behold, there the cottage was, for real before me. I knocked on the door and it opened in a flash. It was Jumping Johnny himself, to be sure, in his shirt sleeves. He invited me in and wanted to know what my business was. I didn't tell him right away. I kept him in suspense for a while.

He was in the middle of making a Christmas cake and he had all the ingredients laid out on the kitchen table They reminded me of a list of declared runners for the Galway Races or Leopardstown. The recipe for this cake was given to him by a lady down the road that he called "Spider Legs" because he said that you could easily knit an Aran Sweater with her spindle shanks.

I apologised for interrupting his domestic and festive season chores. I soon learned that he was a bachelor, living alone and doing his own cooking, cleaning and much more. He offered me a mug of buttermilk but I declined. I then told him what brought me to see him. It was simply, for him to tell me a true story. I felt that he was flattered that I had come a long journey, just to hear a story.

He told me to go out and have a look around the village while it was still bright and that he would tell me a story when I came back and that he would then have the cake in the oven. I agreed to his modus operandi, not wanting to be awkward.

I thought that the village was very much Old World and it was dominated by the mountain and the castle both of which looked scary and weird. There was a zig-zag road leading up to the top with tall dark trees on both sides of the road, closing in at the top to form a kind of canopy. Big black gates confronted you as you came to ascend, attached to hefty pillars that looked ancient and discoloured.

As darkness fell, I returned to Jumping Johnny and by then the Christmas cake was almost a fully–baked product. He said that he was ready to tell me a story, and seeing that I had come so far, he would tell me a local tale. I cocked my ear and away he went. The following is what he told me:

"On the mountain top there are ruins of a castle. That castle has not been inhabited for more than two hundred years. Lord and Lady Henderson-Dawson lived there and they had just one son called Benjamin. They lived the high life, enjoying every luxury, throwing big lavish parties, banquets, going on world tours and inviting "Big Shots" to stay with them.

The furnishings were exotic and they had three grand pianos. They did no work as they had servants, gardeners and farm hands to do the manual work. They lived in quarters downstairs while the Lord, Lady and Benjamin relaxed upstairs. Benjamin was a problem. It seems that he was badly reared and utterly spoiled. He was idle and good for nothing, a proper brat who had no respect for his parents or anyone else. He never had to work, so he turned to mischief of all kinds. He had a fierce temper and could be violent at times.

One night there was a terrible battle between them and it went too far. Benjamin got a heavy axe and killed the Lord and Lady. He then threw them down a long stairway and dragged them into the dungeon, locked and sealed it, so that no one could enter there. Then he spread the news that they had gone on a world tour and that they might not be back as they were retiring to another property that they had in New Zealand.

The local population who knew the nature of things in the castle, were suspicious but did not get involved but a week later Benjamin himself went missing. He would normally be down in the village acting the maggot but there was no sight of him around the place.

Suspicion grew again and two local men went up the mountain to investigate. They looked in through a ground floor window, and what did they see? Benjamin was hanging by means of a rope from a rafter and he was undoubtedly dead. When he did not get his way, not only did he kill his parents, he also took his own life as well.

The police were called in and they found the parents' vault on the castle lands. The news spread quickly and there was a feeling of shock everywhere.

Ever after that, the castle was said to be haunted. The first evidence of that was on the night after the burials, when a brave group of locals went up to the castle. They had seen strange lights in the windows of the castle. They were flashing and coming and going. There was a loud screaming noise as well and figures were seen passing back and over inside the windows which were very large. They heard a sound like glass shattering.

Outside the castle chariots drawn by white horses were seen moving very fast and urged on by two drivers with whips. All of this began after midnight and always on a Saturday night only, the night all three came to the end of their lives. After that, the locals did not venture up there any more as they were scared. One could not blame them.

It was the local people who christened the castle. They added the word "Gurrier" to it because in their opinion a Gurrier lived in it and he was Benjamin Henderson-Dawson. If it were today, they might well give it a different name".

I was grateful to Jumping Johnny for his local tale but refused his invitation to go up to the castle the following Saturday night, to see for myself the goings-on there.

Then I asked him why he had this nickname. He told me that he was a champion at the long jump and the high jump and later he kept horses and used to jump them over the fences at various shows. The local lads gave him his accolade but his real name was Johnny Pooley.

The Irish countryside is dotted with castles, some well preserved and even lived in still. Others lie in ruins. Some castles have been purchased by individuals and families and have been refurbished and modernised. All of them have a long history attached to them. If they could speak, they would have great stories to tell, of days long gone, of banquets, lords, ladies and even ghosts who inhabited the West wing or perhaps, the Dungeon.

Gonzaga Walpole's Letter to her loving Son, Zac

Ballynagat West,
Monday

My dearest Zac,

I hope you got to London town safely. As you will discover, it is a shade bigger than your home village of Ballynagat West but you will get used to it in no time. If you get lost at any point, get on to me, at once, for directions. I have a great head for that, if nothing else.

Now, we are pulling along nicely here at present but, of late, we have experienced many tragedies. Some years are like that. When it rains it pours. You should know that but you were no Einstein going to school. You went down in history but not the way one would like. Still, we were proud of you for your get up and go attitude and your Mamma loves you more than you think.

To come to the tragedies that hit us all here in Ballynagat West. We had a bad thunder storm and Jack the Spark's best cow was killed by lightening over in the long meadow. She was grazing under a big oak tree. She was a great milker and a kind of a pet. They used to call her "Splendid".

Then a car and a truck went into Lake Porcupine near Shuffler's house Saturday night. They sank fast as the lake is very deep at the point of entry.

They say that the drivers were out of their minds with alcohol. You are lucky in that you do not touch that bitching stuff. Four occupants of the vehicles were killed. It was good that they were from another village, twenty five miles from here. It is called Muleville Lower. It would be awful to have to live in a village with that name. You could never hold your head up high. The inhabitants must be an ignorant and awkward lot if one can judge by the name.

Harry the Hammer's daughter, Attracta, passed away yesterday. I hear that it was an overdose of some lethal banned substance. She was a wild one, very silly, not much up on top. To make things worse, Flipper McGrath's lad, only seventeen, took his own life down at the soccer pitch. He was always a bit weird with a stupid grin. It is sad but that's life. It is now a question of living with the dying, but there is some good news as well to cheer us up.

Fat Mary Tom's girl had sextuplets over in the private maternity place in Bawneen. It is very fancy, not a place for the likes of us. It was a fifty-fifty result – three of each. She should be a good deal lighter now. The sale of nappies will increase and maybe the cost of them as well. The village here needs a boost in the population anyway. When she comes home, I must go over to visit and bring her a jam tart. She loves that kind of stuff, signs are on her as she is expanding all the time.

I am not too bad myself, only for the wind which gives me a hell of a time at night. It is a bit like a hurricane and it rumbles through me. The doctor told me to change my diet but that would cost money which I do not have. Maybe when you are properly set up over there, you might be able to rush me a few ginglers, ASAP. Otherwise, it will be water and crusts.

I have gone through a bad patch, of late, with constipation. There was nothing moving at all for ten days so the toilet here was on holidays. My GP gave me a very powerful medication which he said would stimulate movement. He told me to call back to report progress.

Now to come to yourself. I hope that you are looking after yourself. Wash yourself regularly because you suffer from body odour. Fumigate yourself with deodorant and change your shirt and underwear. Scrub your teeth daily, if you have paste, but if not use bread soda, it is more economic. Keep to yourself and do not mix with gurriers, bimbos, drunks or drug addicts. Stick to your knitting. Keep all pressures at bay, now that you are a Londoner.

Before I forget, I know that you will very likely meet Queen Elizabeth. Ye're neighbours. She is a very nice woman and when you meet her tell her that I have great egg-laying hens and that I can send her some large free-range eggs that she could use in her kitchen for baking, scrambling, poaching or simply boiling. Her husband, the Duck of Edinburgh might love them.

I must bring this epistle to a close now as it is running on. Please reply to this, if you can find a bit of notepaper and I will flag you again shortly.

Your problematic Mother, Gonzaga.

Bouncer McGurk on the Fair Day in Cloonfada

Bouncer McGurk has lived through many winters and summers and has a very good knowledge of most things, including the Fair Day in Cloonafada, a day that no longer exists and more is the pity.

As he recalls it, the Fair Day was much more than an occasion for selling and buying animals. It was also a great social event and it occurred once every month. It was a day that all looked forward to and when it came, it was usually enjoyed.

For farmers, fair days were important because they were an opportunity to get some badly needed income from the sales of cattle, sheep, lambs and pigs. Much hard work had gone into rearing the animals so now it was pay-back time, but the prices received were not always great and sometimes, animals were brought home unsold which was a big disappointment.

The animals were taken to the Fair, in the early hours of the morning, frequently, in the dark, especially in Winter. They had to be rounded up by the farmers, with the help of dogs and even the youngsters and they were then walked to the Fair. The men and youths would have long sticks and torches and some dogs also accompanied the animals.

It was common to see men with a long lead on sows and pigs going along the roads. The scene was one of lowing cattle, bleating sheep, barking dogs and one could see the animals' breath rising up in the light of the torches.

As the animals got close to the town, they were met by Buyers or Jobbers, as they were called. Some of them could be from Northern Ireland, others were butchers, all on the look-out for good animals to purchase. Many bargains were made for stock before they ever reached the town.

The unsold animals were taken to the Fairgreen which was anything but green, especially when the weather was wet. It was usually very mucky and dirty and it was difficult to walk around on the surface. It was good that the males were equipped for the weather conditions. They had Wellington boots, heavy overcoats, scarves and either hats or caps, to suit the conditions.

When farms became mechanised, the animals were transported to the fairs in trailers drawn by tractors and some farmers and cattle dealers had trucks or lorries. This took a good deal of the hardship out of getting the animals to the fairs. They then looked much better and it was easier to sell them.

There were certain dramatics attached to selling cattle and they hinged around what was known as making a bargain. The seller would ask a price and the buyer would pretend that it was too high, so he would walk away. He would return again later and ask was the selling price the same. It normally would be, as the seller would not budge from the original asking price. The buyer might then make a better offer if he liked the animals. It would be turned down and he would walk away again.

Sometimes, the buyer might not come back, so the seller might have to come down in price a bit. If the buyer really wanted to purchase, he would appear again and a person nearby who would be watching the goings-on, might suggest dividing the difference between the seller's price and the buyer's offer or the buyer himself might do this. He would then ask the seller to hold out his open hand and he would hit it with his and say: *Will you give them to me at that price* and an onlooker would say: *Go on! Clench the deal, he'll give you a good luck penny* and the final price would be agreed. The "Luck Penny" could be great or small but it was usually part of the bargaining process.

The buyer would then raddle the animals or maybe just lift a bit of manure from the ground on the top of a stick and mark the cattle with it.

It was always a great relief to have sold the stock and then they would have to be held on the fairgreen until the buyer was ready to load them on to his truck or they might even have to be brought to the railway station.

Sometimes they could be brought to a yard and left there for some time until the buyer was ready to take them and of course, one had to wait to get paid for the cattle.

There would be a chance then to get refreshments, food and drink and the youngsters who came to help out, would be very happy to get a bottle of lemonade, sweets and a few coins for themselves.

The sheep, lambs, bonhams and sows were usually kept in pens along the footpaths in the town and the dealings there were more straightforward and simpler, in many ways, as the prices were always much more modest than for good big quality cattle.

There were many side-shows going on which kept people entertained. They were a bit of diversion from the serious business of selling animals. There were musicians playing the traditional stuff, solo singers of doubtful quality, the three-card-trick man, magicians, trick-of-the lube artists, acrobats, guys walking on a platform of glass or nails, or lying down on the broad of their backs, without any concern. There were fire-eaters and jugglers, you name it. They were all there in living colour. The town crier or bellman added his own bit of noise to the scene, informing all present of the events in progress and forthcoming events also.

The Fair Day was not just a man's world. The farmer's wives came to town also and made their own social scene. They would meet friends and neighbours, have a good chat, go into the bars and have nice drinks such as claret, hot port, wine, sherry and even the odd drop of whiskey with water or a hot toddy.

They frequented the restaurants and treated themselves to some good food and then did a bit of shopping before making for home. The Fair Day would keep them going for another month and when the men got home they would hand over the money that they got for the animals to the women so that they could put it away, safely.

Fair Day in Cloonafada was not unlike the fair days in many other towns around the country and when the fairs ceased to be, a great social outlet disappeared. The fun and enjoyment of the bargaining and all the other aspects of the fairs were really missed by many.

The Marts arrived on the Irish scene but they were no substitute for the fairs. They were impersonal and clinical, lacking the social dimensions, fun and enjoyment of the fairs and they were and still are, a man's world because there is not much place in them for women, apart from the ones who have to attend them, to dispose of their animals.

Bouncer McGurk has said it all well and has captured for us, something of the fair days that were. There was some hardship attached to them, but most people who experienced them would agree that they were more a part of what we are, than the Marts will ever be.

Thankfully, there are many films, on record, showing those fairs and if you are a certain age, you might well see yourself, doing your thing, in a fairgreen, on a street in a town or even in a pub.

Going through the countryside today one can see the changes that have taken place in towns since the abandonment of the fairs. The fairgreens have disappeared, in many cases, and new housing estates now stand on the ground where the fairgreens once were. In some cases, even shopping centres or at least various shops have been built on the greens.

Not all towns that had fairgreens developed Marts to replace the fairs. Some of those who did, did not survive, for a number of reasons. In some cases, the Marts were not built on the fairgreen sites but were located some distance outside the towns where sites were available.

Marts, even when in use, are ugly features with all the tubular pens and fencing and so contribute nothing aesthetically to the environment. At least, the fairs were held in green open spaces that always looked pleasant enough except when badly cut up in very wet weather due to cattle and humans walking through them .

All that is left now of the fair days is just the memories and I am thinking of Thomas Moore who wrote these lines:

Oft in the stilly night, ere slumber's chain has bound me,

fond memory brings the light of other days around me.

Breaking News on Radio Funkey FM

Good evening all you idlers out there. You must be idle if you are listening to this Station. My name is Blunderbus X. Featherhead and here now is the latest news from this region, appropriately named Jokerland.

Mary Jane Dot has drawn a line on having any more babies. She has just retired from the activity having recently given birth to a bouncing baby boy, bringing her total to date to seventeen. The decision has disappointed her husband, the little twit, Pimple Toes. He says that he will put pressure on herself to continue as there are still some empty rooms in their mansion of a house. They would benefit from occupancy.

The Tin Hat award has been presented to Paddy Owney Tim for downing twenty-five pints of Guinness, in quick time, in the Stagger Out Bar over in Sturkmore. The only other competitor for the Award was Glugger Gilligan who managed to put away twenty three pints of the black stuff and then gave up on the contest. He said afterwards that it was just as well that he did not win as he had no intention of going around the place wearing a tin hat.

The storm Alfie brought a big heavy tree down on the roof of Kitty Billy Pat's house and squashed it badly. As a result of the disaster, she has lost her head and has not found it since. She was always a bit mad but now she is manic, talking to herself and shadow boxing in her garden. She has climbed up on a tall pillar and is making speeches from there about the state of the country. The lingo she is using may set fire to the damaged property.

Porcupine's daughter has arrived home from Singapore for a short holiday, to chill out, they say. She would need that because she is usually on Cloud 9. Her name is Stitches. She is ninety-five per cent artificial, false this, false that. She walks with her head in the air as if she were tracking an aeroplane in the sky and she has a pronounced swagger. The smart phone never leaves her hand and if you were to meet her on the road, she would not notice you at all. She thinks she is the bees' knees or the Queen of Sheba. She needs to think again.

Twister O'Malley has prescribed a cure for her antics. He says that she needs a kick or two to take the air out of her balloon. He did not say where she is to be kicked, but one can use the imagination or hazard a guess.

Trixie, down in Cloonbeg North bought her first car last week but she is having problems with it. Since it arrived, the locals are out pushing it. It is hard work and it puts a strain on one's system. Chris the Cod remarked that it was a pity when she was going on wheels, that she didn't purchase a yoke with an engine in it. She will learn as she goes along, though some people never learn anything.

The Dog McDonnell died recently and he was noted for his wealth. His property fell to his nephew Poppy Seed and when he took over the place he set to work bulldozing all the old buildings. When he moved in on the cart-house, he had no trouble demolishing it. The day was very stormy and he quickly noticed a huge amount of paper money, Euro notes of all sizes flying around in the wind and being blown out on the road and everywhere. Passers-by thought they were witnessing a miracle. Could this be a new form of the Lottery? The news spread and soon many arrived to see could they pick up some money. The nephew got very angry with them and he hastened to explain that that money was his.

It was in the walls of this cart-house that the Dog McDonald kept his life savings. He did not believe in doing business with Banks or even putting money under the mattress. He never spent much money in his lifetime, skimping and saving and sometimes even starving himself. How stupid he was. He could have had an enjoyable life rather than leaving his wealth for someone else to enjoy. There are probably many more like him, and that is sad.

News is coming in of a fierce altercation between Bumble Bee Moran and Scarecrow Griffin. It is all about a right-of-way and there are varying opinions on the matter. It is not the first time that they had a set-to on this and it is a shame because they are neighbours. The fists were flying and there was no referee. Scarecrow is a big guy and he had no trouble grounding Bumble Bee who is very petit. He went down in the second round and he did not get up. His wife Tiny came on the scene and called the Guards. When they arrived they said that Scarecrow would be appearing in Court, in relation to the matter. Bumble Bee was taken to hospital for reconditioning.

The wedding of the year is taking place today in the church at Japerstown. The bride is Mag Pye and the groom is Jack Dawe. Three hundred guests, of a sort, are attending this Rave and the honeymoon will be spent down in Timbuctoo. Mag is no spring chicken and as regards Jack, with his crooked legs, he has lost count of the number of Christmasses he has put through his hands.

Despite their ages, Jack says, in relation to Mags that he likes the sunshine of her smile. Well, that may be so, but Jack himself has no smile, just a sour puss. The face always looks like we are going to have a fall of snow, or worse still, maybe a hurricane.

Listeners are advised not to visit the village of Bonkerstown West as the sewage system there is not working, giving rise to unflushed toilets and a bad smell has enveloped the area.

Furthermore, all inhabitants there are in bed with a bad flu, bar two souls who have weathered it. One is Caterpillar McGillicuddy, eccentric as hell, odd as forty cats and as cranky as an angry tiger.

He drinks like a fish and loses his common sense, not that that is his strongest point. In fact he is unable to drink without losing his head. He just falls apart and begins talking to himself. He imagines that he is the Agha Khan or the Ayatollah and seems to enjoy this personification.

The other flu-free inhabitant is Blondie Billboard. She lives in another world altogether. The locals call her Split Level. She was married three times and all three husbands died of heart attacks. That tells you something about Blondie. She says that she is now waiting for Godo, in other words, waiting for husband number four. She is hoping to meet a multi-millionaire, not too likely in her God-forsaken village.

She loves birds and has twenty five bird-cages in her house, all Canaries. You can only imagine the chorus that rises up in that homestead. You could call it bringing the environment home. The stress from the birds in the cages could have some connection with the passing of her three men.

News is coming in of a number of happenings over in Tullinageek bog. It appears that the recent, dry, hot weather has started bog fires .There are acres of heather there, full of wild life. Local fire brigades are on the scene applying barrels of water to the flames in an attempt to stop the spread of the fire to nearby buildings and dwellings.

Two of the firefighters have lost their lives as they accidentily fell into a bog-hole filled with water. They are Hairspray Ganley and Mouse Markey, natives of Cloonshock. Luckily, they are single men as there are no single girls living there of an age to marry.

It is also reported that Rags Rafferty has lost his life up at the southern end of the heathland. He was collecting heather to make brooms for sweeping his kitchen. He lost his balance and as he failed to find it again, he was unable to get up off the ground and the flames cremated him .

Finally, a look at the weather. The Met Service says there will be nothing but rain for the next six months, so forget it. There will be no weather, so you can all go off to bed and relax, but we will be expecting you back, to tune in to us again, when you surface.

This is Blunderbus X. Featherhead for Radio Funkey FM signing off. Good night!

Warfare in Puckermore

In the mountainous area of Skirteach there are two small villages. One is called Gorteensalach which is a Gaelic name and in English it means the dirty little tillage field. The other is called Gleann na Muc which translates into English as the glen or valley of the pigs.

These villages are famous for all the wrong reasons, chief among which is the presence in each one of a Gang, both quite dangerous, with no respect for law or order, man, woman, child or beast of the field.

The Gangs are in competition with each other, one trying to obliterate the other. They are into all kinds of rackets, drug pushing, smuggling, scams, robberies, muggings and more. They delight in violence and upheavel.

The Gorteensalachs are known as The Screws and the Gleann na Mucs as The Hatchets. Wherever they show their faces there is trouble and everyone around the area is scared of them. Their numbers have increased in recent times which is not a good trend.

They travel around in vans, selling all kinds of stuff in the more remote parts where they are not well known. They are into furniture, hardware, electrical goods, leather, clothing and many other bits and pieces. Most of which they sell are stolen goods or goods got in some illegal fashion. They are reported as saying that the profits are substantial.

No one opposes them as they are usually heavily armed with guns and knives, not to mention iron bars, hatchets and such like. They pride themselves on their Gangland image and are happy to continue terrorising and conning the public.

Every Summer there is a week-long Carnival in the small town of Puckermore and that is when the factions stage their most daring performances. They usually do their thing on the opening night of the Carnival.

As soon as darkness fell this year, a procession of vans arrived in town. The Screws parked on one side of the main street and the Hatchets on the other.

The occupants of the vans emerged from their vehicles and walked down the town, each faction keeping well apart. They are usually half drunk when they arrive in town and then they enter the pubs and top up for the night.

When they came out again on to the streets, a few guys from each Gang clashed with each other to start a fight and cause a rumpus. At once, the rest of both gangs joined in and then hell broke loose. The fighting was quite fierce for some time. There was pure mayhem all around, a real ruille buille. The language and shouting were vile.

It was not long until weapons of all kinds were introduced. They had iron bars, sticks, stones, knives, hatchets and more. There was a clash of steel in the air and people scurrying for safety. Fists were flying, blood was shed, children were crying, the injured were lying on the footpaths and tarmacadam. The leaders of the Gangs were shouting: *Great stuff. Keep it going.*

When things were at a critical stage, the police arrived and tried hard to calm things down. Big guys from the Gangs moved in and kicked and abused them and then surrounded them, hurtling stones and bricks. Then they produced guns and threatened the police, firing shots up in the air. More police arrived and used their batons and then the Gangs calmed down.

While all this is going on, a marquee was set on fire in another part of the town when cans of petrol were poured around and then a match set the fire off. Shops were looted on some of the side streets and thugs were seen running with boxes, packages, cartons of cigarettes, bottles of wine, crates of beer, and legs of lamb.

In the midst of the mayhem, a battalion of soldiers arrived and flashed their guns. They meant business and the effect that they had was that the feuding factions began to make their getaway, discreetly, as they did not want to be rounded up, taken away and locked up. Luckily, no one was killed but many had minor injuries.

In order to establish peace, of a sort, the leaders of the police and the army brokered a Truce between The Screws and The Hatchets. They said that if both sides abided by the Truce, there would be no further action taken against them, provided they compensated the injured persons and the owner of the marquee. Failing that, there would be summonses, court cases and perhaps jail for many.

In addition all weapons had to be handed over and no member of the Gangs could enter the town, for the next twelve months. All vans had to be removed from the town, without delay.

After that eventful day, the rest of the Carnival days went off peacefully, without disruption and there was nothing heard from either the Screws or The Hatchets for a long time after that.

It was said that both sides observed the terms of the Truce and the small town of Puckermore was left alone to carry on its normal business.

Many adults, especially fathers and mothers of young families said that the violence in the town disturbed the very young kids and they felt the effects of the mayhem for a long time afterwards. They were nervous, had nightmares and would not sleep at night without a light in their rooms and the presence of Mum or Dad with them.

There must have been trouble, though, among themselves, up in the mountain villages. One of The Screws, a guy called The Gorilla was killed in an awful battle with another guy from the opposing faction, The Hatchets. His name was Whiskers. He was supposed to be the daddy of all the Hatchets when it came to viciousness.

Whiskers was into everything that was against the law and it seems that, over the years, he managed to amass a huge amount of wealth. He had property and possessions in many different places and no one dared to touch him. He was looked up to by his Gang as if he were God. He had a wife and she was well able to hold her own as well, not one to argue with, either before or after meals. Her name was Prickly, but the locals called her by another name altogether. For them she was simply The Demon Herself. She had a fierce run in with Turkeycock Cassidy and they both ended in a bloody state. There was no referee on site.

It is not likely now that either side will take a turn for the better. All anyone can do is to steer clear of both Gang members and to always remain vigilant because, with them, you never know the day or the hour that they may strike. It is better to be safe than sorry.

It could be said that feuding factions are not found very often in rural areas of Ireland. They are much more common in the case of the cities where there are large populations and areas of deprivation. Some of them can be very vicious and many murders occur as a result. They are very hard to police and to eradicate. Extra resources and personnel are required to deal with them effectively.

There can be many different causes of feuding factions in urban areas. Some of those involved do not like any kind of competition, so one side tries to eliminate the other. This may have to do with their dealings in drugs, money laundering and claiming areas of operation for their criminality.

Every effort should be made by Governments to eradicate criminality by eliminating the major causes, by way of education, investment in housing, policing and employment in deprived areas.

Cockscomb and Hawkeye: The Unlikely Liaison

By now you must have heard of a lady called Cockscomb, but then, perhaps you may not. Cockscomb of course is her nickname. Her real name is Dolores Matilda Waters. She is generally not liked by the neighbours in her village. Public opinion can sometimes be very hard on people.

She was the youngest in a family of twenty-three. She came late on to the planet but it did not affect her assets. Her poor mother deserved a Nobel Prize for all her labours but that did not happen. Her father was always referred to as Dotty. Mick Sideways described him as not being the full shilling.

Dolores Matilda got her nickname Cockscomb because a woman in the village did not like her way of doing business as she thought that she was of a lower class than herself and she publicised it among the local community in Gawkamore. She said that Dolores was too cocked with her head in the air, too stuck up, too opinionated and she looked down on the rest of the villagers. Jack Paddy Andy put it well when he said that she was dropped in the wrong place altogether. She should have made land in Hollywood, where the Jet-Set hang out.

Cockscomb loved to wear fancy and stylish clothes. She would spend hours in the local towns fitting on gear. She loved gaudy colours and the price did not matter because she was loaded. Before her wealthy aunt died in Australia, she made a Will in which she left Cockscomb all of her money which ran into millions.

One day she was down the village and she happened to bump into a neighbouring woman called Peacock Heatherington and she made some remark about Cockscomb's eye shadow and monster earrings that did not sit well with her. Cockscomb lashed out and bashed her face, so much so, that her colourful decoration required medical attention.

They say that, despite the altercation, they became good friends later on. The situation could have been worse were it not for the intervention of Biddy the Giggles. She had a lovely calming effect which reduced the blood pressure.

For some years, there was a close relationship between Cockscomb and a man in the village called Hawkeye, alias Jack Paddy Mike who was a rough and tumble type, easy going, but not a bad skin. He had a great deal to say and the locals often told him to shut up and put a sock in his gob. He was fairly poor, had little schooling and no job.

One day, he decided to go to America. His father, Flipper, gave him the money to pay his way. He eventually got himself a job in a garage in Boston selling cars. That suited him as he had the gift of the gab. After a while, when he had himself set up and earned a bit of money, he contacted Cockscomb and invited her to the States for a spell. She agreed to go but said that she would pay her own way as she had plenty of dosh. A local Travel Agent booked her flight and she took off for the New World.

Hawkeye was very happy to see Cockscomb on American soil and she updated him on all goings on at home. He took her around the city of Boston and they met many Irish people there who seemed to have got on very well in the U.S.A. Hawkeye was quite happy with his situation but Cockscomb was less so. She missed contact with her buddies back home and one day she rang her best friend in Gawkamore, Nosey McGovern. She could not have rung a better correspondent as Nosey is as good as Reuters, any day. She loves news and loves to spread it around as well. Her preferred material is scandal but failing that, other gossip is acceptable. True to her form, she gave it to her, like this: *The weather is atrocious here, bucketing down every day, floods everywhere. It is great weather for ducks. Johnny Make Do got drowned trying to cross the turlough over in Sliabh Salach. He left twelve kids and an alcoholic wife after him. Scabby Pat's red cow calved. She had twins but a Charolais got stuck in a boghole of deep water and was dead before help arrived.*

Hilda Hogg had quads over in Skint hospital, two boys and two girls. She has ten kids already. She's the one to get the population rolling. Fat Face Finnegan, you know the scientist who lives in Cosy Cottage was carrying out an experiment in his garden, with liquids and gases and there was an explosion. It blew him to bits. Waving Willie's eldest lad, Jinks, overdosed himself with alcohol and drugs and passed away out in his workshop and there is more.

A nasty trick was perpetrated on the old man, Jimmy Marty Joe. The two boyos known as the Pranksters took the engine out of his car a couple of nights ago and when he sat into the car the next day, he was powerless, not a budge out of anything. The poor fellow got a heart attack and died at the wheel. Tough times here. You better stay where you are.

When Nosey had finished her news transmission, she told Cockscomb to ring again in a week but no phone call came for several months. When it did, it was to say that Cockscomb and Hawkeye had got engaged. Nosey was delighted with the news as now she had some work to do, spreading the latest breaking-news around Gawkamore and its environs.

She should not have bothered, because a month later, it was declared off. Cockscomb did not like the idea of having to live in America permanently, so she broke off the engagement. Hawkeye took it badly, went on the booze and drugs, crashed his car and nearly killed himself on the highway. He was left disabled for the rest of his life.

Shortly after, Cockscomb arrived back in Gawkamore and she had learned a great deal from her American experience. She was no longer the head in the air type of woman, the snob, looking down on everyone. No! Life had taught her many things. Life is a very good teacher. She was a new person, humble, accepting, appreciative and glad to be home among people who were, to be fair to them, always kind and generous, with much common sense.

Shortly after her home-coming, she attended a fund-raising event in the local Hall and happened to meet a nice handsome fellow who seemed to like her style. He asked for a date. She agreed and in six months they were engaged. They married a year later in Gawkamore Church, on St. Valentine's Day. Her newly found man was a plumber by trade so he would be able to keep water flowing in her sink. His name was Bertie Cornflour from Ballypickle.

Nosey McGovern was invited to the wedding as were all the locals and she got very drunk so much so, that she had to be carried home by two strong neighbours. Peacock Heatherington was there too, drinking brandy which gave her a fine red face.

The newly weds went off for their honeymoon to the Seychelles. It was a happy ending to a long long saga.

On their return, they were debating as to what enterprise they might undertake. They were undecided, after deliberating for some time. They decided that they would not act until they got advice from some quarter.

One day they walked down the village and happened to meet Ned the Oyster. They stopped for a chat and Ned asked them what were they going to do, workwise. They told him that they could not make up their minds. Ned then said, why not open up a small shop as there was no shop at all in the village or for miles around.

They reflected for a few minutes and then said to Ned that his idea was a good one. They thanked him and returned home. Next day, they employed a tradesman to renovate a big shed that they had and set up a shop, selling groceries, farming, implements, footwear and paraffin oil. It became a success story.

Delilah of Ramstown

The village of Ramstown is where Delilah lives, Delilah Dithering. Of course, the locals rarely referred to her as Delilah. It usually was her nickname that they used. It was easy enough to remember it. It was simply, Gossip. You would understand that wonderfully if you happened to bump into her any day.

One can say that the location of her small bungalow was somehow inspired because it fits in beautifully with her modus operandi or performing style. It is perched on top of a steep hill, painted in brilliant red, with white window frames and a white front door. The view on all sides from atop this hill is magnificent and panoramic in fine clear weather. From this high vantage point one can detect all movements of humans and other objects.

Gossip's residence has another great supporting quality. It enjoys a certain nodality because it is exactly at the crossroads of Ramstown where the various roads run into one another.

You may well ask why I am stressing the aforesaid. The main reason for this is that her location was a tremendous help to her unpaid occupation of minding everyone's business and poking her nose into even the most intimate details of anyone who crossed her path. As one neighbour, Scruffy Scully said: *She is a right bitch for news and scandal. She would go down inside you for information.*

Gossip had a great affection for the school-going children. She used to confront them on their way home from school and confound them with oodles of questions about their home life, parents, relatives and any unusual occurrences.

The older kids were cute enough and didn't give much away but she had a habit of putting the same question to them, a number of times, to see what she could obtain by way of information from them. She often bribed them with lollipops and bulls eyes. Some of them succumbed to her technique.

Her approach was always something like this: *Well tell me this, in your own time, there is no rush. I am not in any hurry.* The kids used to laugh because they thought that she looked very funny. They had a nickname for her house too. They called it "Santa's little home from home in Ireland". The reason for this was its red and white colour scheme.

The older residents of Ramstown did not escape her inquisitive nature either. She was permanent and pensionable in the Corner Shop at the crossroads and she loved news of scandals and any sensational happening. On hearing a tale of any kind, she would immediately put legs on it and exaggerate it to the heights, to a point where the original story was scarcely recognisable.

John Bull who owned the shop regarded Gossip as a menace. One day a fierce fight broke out over some remark she made about John's relations. John wasn't having any of it and opened up. He let fly and demolished her with strong language and clinched fists. He put the fear of God into her. She quickly pulled in her horns and legged it home as quickly as possible. She was lucky to leave the shop with breath in her.

She did walking tours around the area with the ears cocked for news, but sometimes, depending on her mood, she came around riding on her big, old, rusty bicycle which was as heavy and clumsy as a wartime tank. The Duck Finnegan said that it reminded him always of the Iron Age. He felt that some day it could be the death of her.

If you have never met Delilah, alias Gossip, the following may give you some mental image of her for the benefit of your imagination. She is very tall and lanky. There is not a pick of flesh on her, something like the skin and bone dancers that you see performing in Las Vegas. She is undoubtedly ugly-looking. Pakie John Tom, I think got it right when he said that her face resembles a physical map of Siberia in the middle of Winter, icy cold and stern. She is like a telegraph pole on stilts. It is easy to see how no human being ever fell in love with her. One thing is certain. She will never suffer from global warming, whatever else may befall her. Her hair is always tied up in a skyscraper of a bun on top of her head, resembling a television mast. It gets a great buffeting in windy weather and in freezing conditions, as The Dodger Funnyman remarked: *There could even be ice and snow up there.*

When times are quiet in Ramstown, Gossip is sometimes short of ammunition, so she concocts stories of the nastier type and spreads them via the Corner Shop and elsewhere, in the hope of stirring up trouble and to draw attention to herself.

She tagged one piece of scandal on to new arrivals in the village. They had come from Sydney, Australia and they purchased an Irish cottage and a bit of land in Ramstown. The couple and their three children wanted to live in Ireland as their ancestors had come from the Emerald Isle.

Gossip felt that she could do some damage to the new arrivals, commenting that they should have stayed down under and not to be coming to Ramstown to buy up property that should be left to the local people, whenever it came on the market. You see, she was as narrow-minded as hell and deep down, she was malicious. She spread harmful tales around the place and did overtime, meeting as many people as possible to enhance her dirty work. She also travelled farther afield, riding on her rusty two-wheeler to gossip and to discredit the Australians.

In due course, they got wind of what was going on and the man of the house, Alexander, organised a Meeting of the local residents to get some data on her. Alexander had a very fiery temper and would never stand for nonsense or blackmail. Most of those who attended the Meeting supported the newcomers. He was happy with that and returned home to brief his wife and family.

The night of the meeting, Gossip was out of town, so to speak. She had taken off on her magnificent machine to the neighbouring parish of Clutter to gossip with another bird of similar plumage. Her name was Ginks Fecker. She was a Welsh spinster. Surely to God, they were well matched. Both of them had silver tongues, the most exercised organs in their less than exotic anatomies.

Gossip was very late returning as she bagged as much scandal as she could from Ginks and about half way home she got a puncture in the front wheel of the bike, after passing over splinters of glass on the road. It was now very dark and there was nothing for it but to walk home with the ancient rusty mechanism. One is inclined to start singing the late Count John McCormack's famous song: *I'll Walk Beside You.*

When she came as far as the Corner Shop at the crossroads she would have been able in broad daylight, to see her residence high up on the hill, but now it was pitch dark, but she suddenly saw a strange brightness which got more intense by the minute. In the brightness she saw huge flames shooting upwards into the night sky. Night had momentarily turned into day. She stood and stared upwards to where she knew her home should be. She was stunned, shocked and bewildered. Then it struck her. Could her house have gone on fire? Could her worst fear be a reality? Did she leave anything lighting in the house before departing for Clutter?

In no time at all, the villagers of Ramstown emerged from their abodes and gathered at the crossroads, looking upwards at the blazing inferno. Amid the panic, there was no trace of a Fire Brigade to be seen. The smell of smoke was sickening and the dust and cinders were flying around, like a bad attack of midges in a hayfield in Summer time.

Despite her record, the local people felt sorry for her, in her predicament. They rallied around and took her up the hill, on a tractor, to view the disaster.

There was little to be seen, just black walls standing, roof and everything gone. The heat was still intense and some flames rose and fell. As soon as the tractor came to a halt, she dashed in for a close-up view.

She entered where the front door used to be. She picked her steps into where the bedroom was. The bed was gone, mattress and all in which she had banked her life's savings. That was the straw that broke the camel's back or in this case the final curtain, the last hurrah.

With that, Delilah collapsed and fell flat on the smouldering embers. She was down and maybe out, for good. Those who were there took her, with speed, to the nearest hospital, some miles away but she did not recover.

The topic of conversation in the village for some time afterwards was what caused the fire at Gossip's place. After a long investigation, there was no evidence to convict anyone but the rumours were flying about like paper in the wind.

As Fluter McHugh put it: *You can have your own reason for believing certain things happened but you do not have to insist on others holding on to the same view. I have my own opinion and that is good enough for me. You can do likewise, so you can.*

There was great talk all over the place as to the amount of money Delilah had. Some said that she was a millionaire because she never spent much, either on herself or on the house.

Others could not see how she could have much as she never won any money and no one left her any either. Throttle Flynn put it like this: *It's a waste of time talking about her money now. Whatever she had went up in smoke and there will never be any evidence to show what she had. She never went near a bank or a post office in her lifetime. All I want to say is, the rest of you better deal with your finances, in a different way.*

The latest news is that a relative of Delilah has examined the site of the burned down house and is anxious to rebuild the house, in memory of Delilah.

The neighbours are pleased with the move.

Despite this, they still would like to know something about this first secret of Ramstown to set their minds at ease. There is no solid evidence to prove the truth of the rumour that Crazy Bumble-bee Redbottom who once had a serious altercation with the aforementioned Gossip may have been the culprit.

One thing we do know for certain, it was not John Bull in the Corner Shop who burned the residence because he was down in Kerry at the time, enjoying himself at the Puck Fair in Killorglin.

Pimples and Penelope – Mutual Admiration

There is a very remote village, close to the coast and its name is Carraignahulk.

There would not be more than a dozen dwellings in it and they are all huddled closely together with the front door of one facing the back door of another. All the small houses are thatched, with a single chimney emitting plenty of smoke into the sky overhead.

Carraignahulk is as rural as you will get and two houses in the village stand out and catch the eye. The most impressive thatched cottage is that of a man known as Pimples. He is regarded as the King of the settlement.

I can hear you asking: "Why is he called Pimples?" You would not have to ask that question were you to meet him in the flesh.

His entire face is covered with pimples and they have been with him from childhood. As Rickety Dick remarked: *His dial is like a garden of ripe strawberries all ready for harvesting.*

Pimples' cottage is painted in deep purple, which in itself gives it a kind of royal touch. It has been enhanced by a lovely rose garden in front, with a low evergreen hedge surrounding it.

Pimples is a bachelor but despite his age, now, sixty nine, he is always open to accept an offer of marriage, should the right type of lady ride into town.

The other eye-catching cottage in Carraignahulk is that of an aged single lady whose name is Penelope. Her cottage has a deep golden shade of masonry paint, commented on, especially by The Clout Murphy. He says that her house always reminds him of a beautiful sunset.

Penelope herself is a nice warm, pleasant and happy woman, always cheerful, welcoming and very generous. She is regarded as the Queen of the village and she has a soft spot for Pimples but though they have known each other and have been friends for thirty years, they have never decided to marry. Mug the Monk said they prefer to be free-wheeling and like just looking at one another. It costs nothing.

Pimples has a favourite song that he sings, in the vicinity of Penelope's house. You know the one that goes *I'll take you home again Kathleen.*

When Penelope hears it, carried by the wind in her direction, she just shakes her head and smiles broadly. When Pimples calls to her house he delays somewhat and she makes tea for him and always gives him a plate of ham and tomatoes, followed by some of her homemade sweet-cake as she is a super home baker.

Her soda bread is greatly sought after in the locality. She has her own recipe which she keeps to herself. Regina the Ripper has tried hard to get it from her but to no avail. Her comment then was: *Her bloody recipe is as precious as the Crown Jewels. Well, she will not be able to bring it with her when she exits Planet Earth for the lift-off to the next realm.*

If Pimples calls to her late in the evening, the Menu is different. It is supper-orientated, so he gets hot milk or hot chocolate or Horlicks and a slice of her renowned soda bread. The result is that the good man goes home full and happy and Penelope herself feels good as her generosity has been exercised.

She has another hobby which is very dear to her heart. She is a prize-winning knitter. All of this skill, she learned from her mother, popularly known as Stitches. She has won prizes in competitions and now she gives lessons on knitting to the school-children and they love them. Pimples has not been left out of the knitting world because Penelope has knitted two lovely bawneen jumpers for him so he has no excuse for being cold in the Winter months. He says now that he is as good as the late Clancy Brothers and Tommy Makem but that he is unable to do the music bit, for technical reasons.

Pimples has other special interests to keep himself busy. He has a few acres of land and keeps twenty-five donkeys on them and sells them off throughout the year. They are a varied lot, some black, some white, some grey, some brown, and even some with mixed colours, multi-coloured you could say. At times they all join in and give the locals what Jamjars calls *The Asses Chorus* from Pimpey, with apologies to the great classical composers of other days. Well, when they start up they would drive you mad with their Hees and Haws, Haws and Hees. Ear plugs are recommended.

He had one bad experience with a donkey he called Frisker. The said animal knocked him down on the ground one day and then fell on top of him. The poor man thought that that would be the end of him. He recited a Litany but it was not of the Saints.

He struggled and managed to pull himself up off the ground and from under the donkey. He was very shaken by the encounter. A neighbour, Knobs McCool came along and learned of the mishap. He consoled and comforted Pimples as best he could and as he always carries a bottle of whiskey in his inside pocket, he gave him a shot of it and it worked wonders.

The man's courage was restored and Knobs's last words to him were: *That donkey is a dangerous bastard and should be shot on the spot.* Pimples was more kind to him and did not follow Knobs's advice but he did sell the animal later, to a Circus owner who would probably have trained him up for other activities.

I nearly forgot to tell you that Pimples plays cards every night during the Winter. He has won many prizes including money, pigs' heads, crates of Guinness and beer, bottles of wine and whiskey and many vouchers. They were won playing Twenty Five. When playing that game, he is completely honest and above board.

When he turns to his other great game which is Poker, he changes his tactics and becomes the supreme cheater, never showing his cards, never accepting that he can lose. He creates major problems for those who play with him.

His performance at Poker is out of keeping with his usual behaviour but maybe it pays off because he always takes the stakes and there is no comeback. This is the one blot on his copybook but he is quite happy to be regarded as the Poker Champion of Carraignahulk, irrespective of how the title has been secured.

The locals are now expecting an announcement relating to the possible wedding of Pimples and Penelope as he was spotted in a jewellery shop as if purchasing a ring. There is no solid proof of this as it is just rumour.

The wisest old woman in the village, Biddy Stew has put it well: *Let ye not be silly. That pair will never sleep in the same bed because they are happy and content as they are, admiring each other for the last thirty years. That's mutual admiration and it goes nowhere.*

I think I will leave the last word to Biddy, and you know, she is most likely right.

The Cuckoo McDonnell has a different view. He remarked that he had seen Penelope in one of the stores in Quackmore looking at beds and bedding and that could be a sign of some kind of progress in the romance stakes. She was also singing but that could be due to an intake of some alcoholic liquid. Only time will tell what will happen but if they do not hurry up, they will have left this world for the great beyond.

Time moves on and our pair have taken a step closer to nuptials, or is that only a guess? It is a fact that they have hired a hackney man to drive them as they are having a day out. They have briefed him well, in advance. The latest news is that they are taking in the views on the Cliffs of Moher.

Pakey and Festy in Conversation

Pakey and Festy live in the same village and they are there for a long time. They went to school together and ever since they have been great pals. They live alone and the thought of marriage never entered their heads or if it did they made no move to give us any evidence of nuptials.

The village in question is Crookedfield and our two boys live next door to each other. That is very convenient for them as they visit each other every night for a conversation, on various topics of the moment. They have no time at all for radio or television. They say that they do not want to be corrupted by all the nonsense that goes on in the media. They say it could seriously damage their mental health and more.

Last Friday night they got together for a chat but not before they ate two good dishes of organic porridge, well lubricated by milk from the nearby shop. The following is a correct version of their conversation.

Pakey:	Hello Festy! Welcome to my nest tonight.
Festy:	By the looks of it, it will make a dirty night.
Pakey:	It will! It is the time of year for anything.
Festy:	Any news around the place today?

Pakey: Mary The Wag had triplets last night.

Festy: By heavens, she did it in a big
way, so she did.

Pakey: She did! That is her form.
everything she does, she does
it in a big way.

Festy: She does! She is a big woman
herself and is not showing any
sign of being through a
famine.

Pakey No! That brings the family size
To eleven, very big by today's
standard.

Festy: Very big indeed! They can now
form a soccer team all by themselves.

Pakey: They can but they do not have the record for
it yet because "Wild Rick" and his wife have
twenty two, at the last count, up there in
Puddlemore.

Festy: Well, do you tell me. Strange in a way, for
Wild Dick is only a miserable little squirt of
a man but herself, Tina Jizz covers far
more land area.

Pakey: You have hit the nail on the
head.

Festy: Jack the Dart's son has just arrived
back from Hong Kong. He works
in a toy factory over there. He
was always wild, a bit of an
idiot and he fancied himself
going around with his shiny
shoes and long hair down his
back like a monkey.

Pakey: He was a spoiled brat, badly
reared. I hope he is not home to stay.
We have enough of his type around here.

Festy: True enough but did you hear
about the bucks down the road
that broke into banks over in
Scollopbeg ?

Pakey: No! I missed that one. What
happened?

Festy: They were caught red-handed
by the Gardaí.
They have them in custody.
They are on drugs and wanted
to get handy money to
buy supplies. They were always
into criminality.

Pakey: A story I did not miss was when
Marrowfat Fogarty won a
Million in the Lottery last week. She nearly
passed away with excitement. She never had
a penny to her name before that.

Festy: Winning that kind of money would go to
your head and probably destroy you.

Pakey: You have it right there but she is married to
a man who will revel in it. He is a full-blown
spare wheel if there ever was one. He will
soon get through the million if he gets his
hands on it.

Festy: I heard that Marrowfat herself is going on
a world tour but it is unlikely that she will
shell out to bring Dick Head himself. He
would get lost in Australia or Hawaii or
somewhere foreign. He is awful stupid.

Pakey: I was down in Magoo's shop and when I came outside I saw Whiskers Finnegan whizzing past on his rusty old bike, head up in the air and several bags tied tightly on the carrier. He seemed to be on a mission.

Festy: Spot on! He goes over to the village of Thone South to his aging sister, Pearly Ears and he brings her provisions. She has only limited mobility.

Pakey: Good for you he kept going because had he come to a stop he would hold you up for the rest of the day. He can be a bit of a pain in the cold of Winter and even in the heat of the Summer.

Festy: You know of the Kangaroos, Limpy and Seedy. They were in Dubai for some time and are now home to stay. They were saying that they did not like the heat out there and that it was a dangerous place.

Pakey: I remember the day they got married over in the church in Boartown. It was a belter of a wet day and I was perished with the cold. The guests at the wedding were saying that the bride was a bit lame but The Joker Murtagh made light of it and said that Seedy did not marry Limpy for jumping ditches.

Festy: Well, Pakey, it is a point of view. Too bad about poor old Smack Mongan. He was a gentle soul but if he took drink, he could boil over.

Pakey: Did you get the correct details of what happened?

Festy: I made it my business to get the facts. He was over in Waspville and went into the pub there called The Staggering Inn. He met a few of his old-time buddies and drank a belly full of what was going, forgetting all about how he was to get home. He eventually sat into his vintage vehicle and gave it wind as he was feeling very brave after the night on the liquid. He was not too familiar with the narrow winding roads and suddenly fog began to rise, making driving conditions difficult. Visibility was greatly reduced and it seems that the road turned and Smack did not, so he ended up in the deep River Rash and could not exit the vehicle. The poor fellow was drowned but, at least, he had a good night out in Waspville.

Pakey: Too bad! It was the drink that did him in but the fog did not help the situation either. May his soul rest in peace. It is getting late so now it is time for our own nightcap. I have a bottleen of very good stuff here and we will have a slug of it. It is the right kind of thing to have in your stomach just before you go to bed.

Festy: You heard about Jack the Knack, I suppose. All his expensive tools were stolen the other night. He had them in a trailer, parked outside his residence. He will never learn anything.

Pakey: You would want to bring them to bed with you nowadays. They would steal the shirt off your back. They knew what was worth taking.

Festy: Some thug grabbed Jiving Julia's handbag
on the footpath outside Kinky Kitty's hair salon
yesterday and made off with it.

Pakey: What kind of things would she have in her bag,
I wonder, probably bits of junk.

Festy: She didn't tell me but she had €500 in it.
It's late. I'm off. Thanks for the hospitality.
I didn't mean to keep you up so late but we
had a big Agenda to cover. It is a challenge to
keep ahead of things, that's for sure.

Pakey: Good night, Festy.
See you tomorrow!

Suasa and Síosa – Girls Apart

When the millionaire retirees, Zac and Trixie Redwater died over in the village of Ballydoodle North, they had left their estate and mansion to their two daughters, nicknamed Suasa and Síosa. Their real names were Alyson and Amanda.

The Mansion was divided up between them, Suasa inheriting the top storey and Síosa the bottom storey. The estate was likewise divided, the half next the Mansion which was the best land was left to Sousa and the half that was more remote and of lesser quality, landwise, went to Síosa, not that it made much difference as neither was interested in farming.

This Upstairs-Downstairs combination was as different as the two ladies themselves, who were a chalk and cheese duo. Sousa upstairs was very good looking and handsome, quite tall and having a big consignment of long blond hair which went well down her back. Her fashion was elegant, purchased in the leading fashion stores. Money was no problem because she had stacks of it. She wore very strong perfume, the scent of which would knock you down. It cost a fortune to purchase it but it was what the lady wanted.

She never dirtied her hands with household chores or any other kind of work. She did not have to because she had a Chef and four maids to carry the can for her. Some people would tell you that she was badly reared, a spoiled child and now as a grownup, a good for nothing. Big Willie McGurk, a neighbour, living near the Manor, summed her up well: *She is just sitting in her grandeur with all her wealth, waiting for some rich fool to come along and take her off the shelf. Well, I hope, should such turn up, that he will have the cop-on to leave her stewing in her own fat, not that she has much of that either.*

Suasa has a leaning towards parrots and the entire upper part of the Mansion is infested with these talking birds. They are all in cages and they hang in no particular order from hooks in the woodwork, along the corridors and elsewhere. If you like constant noise this is the place for you. If not, do not enter as you would very likely commit suicide before long. These exotic birds come from many parts of the world and they sport some magnificent colours. They speak in different tongues and are outstanding mimics. Jack the Ass calls the upper mansion a lunatic asylum and he may be right. It is certainly not a place to visit if you want to chill out or put the feet up.

Because the Estate lends itself to outdoor pursuits and because there are numerous stables well fitted out, Suasa has invested in several horses. This is the reason for having a great liking for riding, not that she is much good at that. She has fallen off horses at least ten times and has been lucky that she did not break a limb.

Síosa who lives downstairs in the Mansion has no airs or graces. She is very grounded and according to one who knows her well, Jack Dawe, she is in every way, the standard type of woman as against Suasa who is an example of the deluxe model.

Síosa is of small stature, rotund, heavy and almost as wide as she is high. She would never win a beauty competition but can be quite pleasant and light-hearted, with a good knowledge of current affairs both at home and abroad. She is an avid reader of various types of books and has her own special hobbies to which I will now refer briefly.

She has a great love of cats and when you get close to the Mansion you can see cats of all sizes and colours running here, there and everywhere. You can smell them, too, and it would seem to me that no mouse or rat would come next or near this precinct. She lays out special foods for them in little trays and even saucers of liquid to drink. In the garden she has a big Cats' Tent which has lighting at night. It looks like a Five Star haunt, so it is good to be a cat in this place. I wondered have these cats a Trade Union. Day or night, the cat sounds are everywhere and now and again you can hear an out of tune chorus of weird noises. Síosa knows them all by name and many of them are amusing such as Monster, Skinny, Twitty, Splash, Pudding, Blondie, Scamp, Rascal, Knacker, Busty, Cranky, Dusty, Fluffy, Fairy, Foxy, Grumpy, Lanky and so on.

I have not been in the vicinity of the mansion for some time, so recently, I decided to make a journey to the area which is called Hoggetstown. It is a nice enough piece of countryside, dotted with small lakes, patches of evergreen trees and mountains in the distance. The land looks well cared for and the houses are also well kept.

I popped into the local hotel and mingled with some local people who were in the Bar having a drink. I drew down the mansion to see could I glean any information relating to Suasa and Síosa. One very chatty lady who looked obese quickly updated me. My ear was cocked to record every tittle of news. Suasa, she said, met a wealthy oil baron from Texas called Alex. He had come to the mansion in search of his roots, as his people before him had hailed from Hoggetstown.

He fell for Suasa and it seems she fell for him. They married and went off on a luxury Caribbean Cruise. All was well until they returned home. In no time at all, he got very contrary and unsettled. It was not so much Suasa that was troubling him but the parrots. They had him demented and he wanted to get rid of them. Suasa would not agree to his request. The battle began and continued for some time.

Alex sought some escape from the mayhem and ended up most days and nights in the local pub, drinking enough and one could say, too much. He used to stagger home and one night he lost his way and walked into one of the little lakes in the area. The cold water woke him up and he realised his predicament.

When he arrived home Suasa opened up and in no time his ears were hot from the tongue-lashing he got.

He learned no lesson because later on, he turned to drugs and one evening he took an overdose and died. As a result of the tragedy Suasa packed her bag and said goodbye to the mansion and to Hoggetstown. She left the country and settled instead in Monte Carlo where she purchased a fairly modest residence and continues to live in blessed solitude near the Mediterranean water's edge.

A chatty lady told me that she is now involved with Motor Racing and she visits the Casino there to gamble a few Euros. No better place, I said, for both operations. She concluded by saying that the upper part of the mansion was now lonely and desolate and all the parrots are gone. There was an outbreak of some strange disease and it swept them all. At least, peace now reigns within the marble halls and perhaps a ghost or two may have taken their place.

I thanked the chatty lady for her information and as she was watching the clock for some appointment I did not detain her further. The proprietor of the pub told me her name was Gonzaga Bonkers but the locals always referred to her as Gonzo.

Before I left the pub I was anxious to learn something of Síosa and I was lucky in that the local journalist was there having a coffee. I struck up conversation with him after buying him a large brandy. He reported news under the pen-name of "The Wagger". He lived in a village nearby called Scroungeville. He knew of Síosa in the mansion and he said that she did a line with a local photographer who had a great love of animals. He had forty five pets between rabbits, hares, doggies, piglets, lambs and of course cats. He fell in love with more than Síosa. He loved her army of cats as well.

The pair of them tied the knot, so to speak and for their honeymoon they went on a Safari to Africa. There, they were fascinated by the Wild Life and on their return to Hoggetstown they decided to develop a big Zoo, a project they brought to fruition, in a short space of time.

Did they have any family? I asked. The Wagger replied that Síosa had Quads – two boys and two girls. That guaranteed heirs to the grand mansion of Hoggetstown. The wind was on their backs and they were good sensible workers. They refurbished the mansion and employed local people to work on the Estate lands, giving rise to a thriving enterprise. They exuded a nice community spirit and were liked by all the neighbours.

I was grateful to "The Wagger" for his update and in a flash, he was out the door in pursuit of some breaking news in the area. I believe the glass of brandy improved his flow of speech and it might also have sharpened his memory.

When I left the pub, I sat for a while in my car reflecting on the two sisters, Suasa and Síosa, both birds of a different feather. Suasa, the upstairs model, an elegant lady, rich and sophisticated, but also idle and disorganised, lacking in push, drive and ambition, did not make the best of decisions in life. The spoiled child did not quite measure up to what one would have expected from a wealthy aristocrat.

By comparison, her downstairs sister, Síosa, ordinary, just standard in many ways, frugal, plain-living, hard -working but with much common sense and business acumen, did a great deal better. Some people do justice to their talents by using them while others go through life without even noticing the talents they were given. The old people used to say that you cannot always judge by appearances or take the book by the cover. What do you think? Would you agree with them? I do.

Joe Pat Tom and Flicker

Recently, my wanderings took me to a village called Prigstown East which implies that there must be another village called Prigstown West, but I did not venture there as I had heard bad things about it. I just gave it a wide berth.

I met a local man who asked me did I hear the latest local news. I said that I had not heard so he proceeded to update me, immediately.

He told me that Joe Pat Tom lives down the road here and he got a letter the other day saying that his sister who has lived in Miami, Florida for the past forty years, is coming home to see her mother who lives with Joe Pat and she is coming home for good as she has retired from her occupation as a cookery expert, of sorts.

This news is worrying both of them as they know that their visitor is likely to be hard to live with as she is the most unusual specimen of human being, in many ways. They do not want to be stuck with her permanently.

She is due to hit land on Saturday so Joe Pat Tom is busy cleaning up the house and the surroundings. He is cursing and swearing that he has to exert himself for the sister who rates at or below zero with him.

For your information, her name is Flicker and you know it is good because she certainly lights up at times, in all the wrong ways, according to Joe Pat Tom. He thinks that she is half mad or more than that.

Flicker is what he calls an Old Maid as she never married but she stacked up the dosh but never gave any of it to poor Joe Pat Tom. She worked for a long time in Las Vegas, Nevada before going to Florida.

Joe Pat and his mother said that they would try to weather the storm, at least, for a short while but if things got really bad he said that he might have to shoot her or take an overdose of something himself.

Saturday arrived and so did Flicker on an early morning flight into Shannon Airport. Joe Pat Tom was there to meet her, but in very bad mood and quite edgy and contrary. He thought that he would have trouble recognising her but he need not have worried because our bold lady of Miami came bouncing into the arrivals hall, waving an American flag in one hand and then she exchanged it for a placard with the name Flicker in large print upon it. She was sporting a huge red hat with big long feathers standing up on the top like a television mast. She was singing at the top of her voice *The Last Rose of Summer* before she broke into – *When Irish Eyes are Smiling.*

The following day she awoke to the sound of barking dogs because Joe Pat Tom had four of them to help him with the livestock on his small farm. She tore down to the kitchen and did several war dances in the middle of the floor. She was hopping mad as she was awake all night with the barking dogs and worse than that was the fact that she was shivering with the cold. The transition from Miami to good old Prigstown was having an effect on her.

You see, there was no central heating in the house and when the turf fire went out, at night, the arctic conditions set in. She attacked poor Joe Pat and left him feeling awful. She reduced him to cinders. She immediately instructed him to contact a heating firm to install a proper heating system in the house but she made it quite clear that she would not be footing the bill for it.

Joe Pat Tom was distraught as fierce outlay was required for the work, but for the sake of a peaceful existence he complied with her wishes. He paused for a break and then went to his own private cupboard, took out a bottle of good brandy. He drank a glass and then another glass before he got into action.

Next move, Flicker told him to quit the kitchen cooking as she was taking over the culinary requirements of the residence. Joe Pat had lost another round but that was not all, by a long shot.

The next thing that caught her eye was the toilet. It was not a deluxe model and was uncomfortable for sitting on, she said. She told Joe Pat Tom to get a plumber to replace it. With that he walked out in the fresh air for some relief.

The next target was the mother. Flicker told her to tidy up, wash herself and change her clothes. She asked her for some of her pension money and then belted off to a drapery shop in Slabtown and purchased some new apparrel for the mother. On her return, the mother took one look at the purchases, then gathered them up and threw them into the garbage bin. She told her daughter that she was not quite ready for the theatre or the circus and had no intention of becoming a prima donna or a clown, for that matter.

Flicker reddened and fire came into her eyes. She put words on more than the Ten Commandments and ranted and raged to the point where the mother fainted but came too again and then went off to bed without her supper.

When Joe Pat returned after booking a plumber Flicker packed him off again to town, to order a new kitchen as she said that the kitchen in the house was not fit for purpose. She could not show off her cookery skills with it, so it had to go.

He was almost at breaking point now and began talking to himself in a language no one would understand. He revved up and as a result, some novel words were uttered and were well-spoken by His Lordship. Whatever Flicker got that day, it wasn't a blessing. He said he hoped that when the kitchen would be installed that she would burn herself to cinders in it.

The expense of it all was beyond him and she would not pay a penny towards anything, despite her demanding nature. At the end of the day he had to sell off some cattle and sheep to get money to pay his bills and he was livid that this awful woman came into his house and his life and destroyed his peaceful and easy-going existence, causing him to spend and spend money that he could not afford.

One night Flicker went down to the only pub in the place and there she got into a conversation with an elderly gentleman by the name of The Weed Scully. She liked him and he seemed to like her, not really knowing her inbuilt qualities. The meeting led to another and soon she visited his house and liked what she saw there. It was quite luxurious in many ways.

Joe Pat Tom got wind of the liaison and was thrilled to think that, maybe Flicker could be off-loaded and then someone else could do the suffering, rather than he. Time would tell.

Flicker 's mother was a very quiet woman, very easy-going and she was also wise in that she never became involved in an argument with the daughter and she did not cross her, in any way. She had her own opinions about her but kept them to herself.

After some time the romance came to a good conclusion. Flicker announced that she was moving in with "The Weed" in a week's time. Joe Pat said nothing out loud until she had packed her bags and moved out of the house. Then he took down the old gramophone, put on a record of Irish Dance Music and danced to his heart's content on the kitchen floor. He performed two reels, three hornpipes and four jigs and the mother joined in. The bottle of brandy came out and both had a large glass to celebrate liberation from a real pest. It really was their lovely day. Joe Pat went down on his knees and thanked the Lord for the release.

As to whether the pair lived happily ever after, your guess is as good as mine. Joe Pat said that, that scenario was highly unlikely. One thing is certain, he and his mother did.

Mamma Phones Her Son Jacko

Mamma:	I can hardly get a minute, nowadays to try and call him, now that I have a few minutes to myself. I'm dialling! Hello Jacko, are you there?
Jacko:	Hi Mamma! I'm fine. How are you? It is good to hear you on the blower.
Mamma:	I'm not great. The Winter was tough. My arthritis is acting up. The pain is killing me. It is old age I suppose.
Jacko:	You should go to the Physio and do exercises.
Mamma:	Good advice. I must go when I get a chance.
Jacko:	Are you well otherwise?
Mamma:	Not at all! I suffer from bad indigestion and I am terribly constipated, you know, not being able to do anything when I go to the toilet. Of course, my bunions are getting worse by the day, not to mention the migraine.
Jacko:	You should try Rennies for the indigestion and laxatives for the other thing, to loosen you out, combined with exercising. Go to the chiropodist to sort out your feet

problems and take paracetamol for the migraine. You have to be on top of things, all the time.

Mamma: Thanks for your tips. Another problem I have is bad wind in the tummy. It is continuous, morning, noon and night. It sounds like a hurricane, a mighty wind blowing inside me. Shaking Sally recommended taking bread soda and ginger for that. To tell the truth, my dresser is more like a well-stocked pharmacy.

Jacko: Well, at least you have some remedies and that is a good thing.

Mamma: Now there is another thing bugging me. I am unable to sleep at night and when I take sleeping pills I wake up and go walking in my sleep, if you can call it sleep at all. Next day, I am flat out on the couch looking into space.

Jacko: You should see your GP for advice. Do not overdo the pills or you might not wake up at all.

Mamma: I am careful enough but as you know I am addicted to whiskey which I drink every day and night. It could be interfering with my medication.

Jacko: That could be so. I think you should cut back on the spirits, for a while. Try something less potent such as Ginger Ale or maybe Red Bull for a boost,

	now and again for variety.
Mamma	How are things with yourself?
	Are you earning any money? The
	cost of living is very high in Paris.
Jacko:	It is, but I am doing well. I got a job
	in the Ritz Hotel. It is very posh and
	big wigs book in there every day all
	well-heeled. The grub in it is super.
	I do well on tips.
Mamma:	I am delighted to hear that. Where is
	your accommodation?
Jacko:	It is beside the River Seine and Notre Dame Cathedral.
Mamma:	That sounds very nice to me. Pop
	into the Cathedral and say a prayer
	for me, for my health problems.
	Have you seen much of the city?
Jacko:	I have seen all the big features such
	as the Eiffel tower, the Louvre, the
	Arc de Triomph, the Champs Elyssey
	and Rue de Bach. It is a very big city,
	unlike our home place –
	Ballypraiseach.
Mamma:	That is good to hear. Have you
	learned any French?
Jacko:	Lots, Mamma. Bon Jour! Bien Venue!
	Tres Bien! Si Vous Plait.
Mamma:	Your French is impressing me. Have
	you met President Macron yet?
Jacko:	Not yet but it is early days.
	Any big news in Ballypraiseach?
Mamma:	Any amount, mostly bad news. We
	seem to have a great deal of misfortune.
Jacko:	Tell it as it is, Mamma. Let it roll.
Mamma:	Mary Jane Dotte crashed her motor

bike down at the Luper's Bridge. She broke her hips and had to get steel ones fitted instead. She's a heavy lump. As of now, she is grounded.

Jacko: She was always a bit of a hazard on the road, reckless I would say. The school children were scared of her when she catapulted down the booreen to the main road.

Mamma: We had seven break-ins, of late. Patsy Suds O'Hagan was beaten up by thugs and he was robbed as well. He is in hospital and may not survive. He is nearing a hundred.

Jacko: They should be locked up for life.

Mamma: I nearly forgot to tell you about Jenny Daffodil McGrath. She was at Mass down in the Church and after lighting candles, her clothes caught fire and the flames and smoke were horrifice. The Hedgehog Reilly was in the Church and he witnessed the spectacle. He said that it reminded him of Moses and the Burning Bush. He did the Good Samaritan, got a fire extinguisher and sprayed the fire. Jenny's clothes were destroyed but she suffered only minor burns.

Jacko: Candles aside, Jenny was always a fiery piece of goods, for sure.

Mamma: The Gawk Nolan is in jail. He raided an ATM, smashed it open with a hatchet and made off with thousands of Euros. The Guards caught up with the scoundrel and had him put behind bars.

Jacko He was always into criminality, a bad yoke. Have you any good news at all?

Mamma: Yes! Your father won €5,000 Euros in a Draw down in the local Hall. He said he is going to send you a bit of his winnings. I hope he sends it before he has it all spent on drink.

Jacko: Tell me more, Mamma.

Mamma: The pair we used to call the Ginger Nuts got married last week. They were walking out together for twenty six years, no rush there. Rocking Ricky remarked about them that both Vinny and Assumpta had great mileage on the clock and would be entitled to a scrappage allowance, but then perhaps they might get into the Guinness Book of Records.

Jacko: Wonders never cease. That's a kind of chalk and cheese combo.

Mamma: The Yank McMahon is home from the States, to stay. He is building a mansion down near Stuffy Nora's place. It will have swimming pools, spas, hot tubs and jacuzzis. He used to be going around with rags of clothes and the father was a wreck, with broken down shoes and holes in his trousers.

Jacko: He must have done well in America. I might be able to buy him out some day.

Mamma: Before I finish, Laughing Larry who has spent his lifetime drinking in the local, you, know, the Quaking Tavern, is gone completely deranged and he is so bad that he now laughs all the time and keeps singing- *Danny Boy.* When he is distracted, he sets into another ditty – *We Won't Go Home Until Morning.* Of course, he never did go home from the pub until morning, only to break for breakfast.

Jacko: It is tragic what drink can do to a person. I have to go now, Mamma, as my work shift is beginning shortly, but before I go I want to tell you that I have a girlfriend. She's French, naturally, and I fancy her. She likes me, too.

Mamma: Well, you are a fast mover. I hope she is not a bimbo. Has she any class?

Jacko: She has great class. Her parents live on the French Riviera. They are filthy rich and she works in the French Embassy.

Mamma: I like the ring of that. Good lad! What's her name?

Jacko: Her name is real French. She is Juliette, you remember Shakespeare's *Romeo and Juliette.* She was the heroine in it. The name means youthful, beautiful and vivacious. I'm off! Ring again soon for a tongue wag.

Mamma: Hold on a minute! I nearly forgot to tell you more that you might like to hear. As you know, I am very forgetful now. My old head is in need of a service so it is like other heads in the family.

Jacko: Never mind! Your head is better than some people I know. Now, tell me the good news.

Mamma: Your Auntie Flathead who lived in her little cottage down in the village of Killnaheehaw died some time ago and as she was a spinster she never spent much money either on herself or on anyone else. She always banked any money she got. She was a dressmaker.

Jacko: The suspense is killing me. What is the good news, Mamma?

Mamma: Well, before she cocked her clogs or whatever she was wearing at the time, she made a Will and left you some dosh. I am unable to say any more now as I want it to be a surprise when you come home for a visit.

Jacko: That will not be long, Mamma. I'm away!

Mamma: That's great news. I like your style. Cheerio for now and be careful in the Paris traffic.

The Big Snow of 1947

There is a house down there in a place called Fairyville where the locals play cards, mostly Twenty Five, but sometimes Poker. I joined them recently for a game and enjoyed it greatly.

When we had finished card-playing the woman of the house – Cissie – made tea and sandwiches for all present. She is a very decent and generous woman and there is plenty of her in it as well. If she happened to fall on top of you, you would experience considerable pressure on your anatomy.

There was great talking done and much reminiscing about times past. I was sitting beside a very chatty lady, called by the locals "Spindle Shanks", a kind of opposite number to the woman of the house. The locals are great for nicknames and they seem to get a kick out of using them. They say that it is all just for fun.

She broke into talk about the big snow of 1947. She lived through it and had vivid memories of that terrible time.

I asked her to go easy so that I could make some notes and she willingly obliged. I may not have brought every detail with me, but what I did may evoke memories in those who lived through the misfortune themselves.

There was snow in January and early February but it was not too bad, but the real blizzard struck on the 24th February. It was due to an Arctic depression which was very severe. It was bitterly cold with a strong easterly wind blowing. Snow fell continuously for about 48 hours, worst in Munster and Leinster at first and later in Connaught and Ulster.

The amount of snow that fell was unprecedented. There were snow drifts seventeen feet high in places and even where there was less snow, the drifts were six or seven feet deep. The entire country came to a standstill. Everything was under snow. Walls, fences and gateways were not to be seen. Roads and railways were blocked and covered in deep snow. The trees in their white icy covering were truly magical.

Coming only a couple of years after the end of World War II, Ireland was not in good shape to deal with it. Towns-people were closer perhaps to shops and supplies of food than rural dwellers but then, in time, the shops were running low in provisions because many roads and railways were not operational. At that time much food and other supplies came by rail and it took time to open the rail links and indeed the roads themselves.

People themselves did their best to clear the snow from around their houses. They opened up pathways to essential locations but it was all very hard cold work.

In rural areas, farmers had a good deal of food on the farms such as potatoes, turnips and other vegetables but because the land was frozen to a great depth they were unable to open up holes of potatoes or turnips or whatever, for use. They had milk, butter and eggs and some would have meat, more likely bacon, as many killed pigs then.

Those were the times when there was severe rationing of many foodstuffs and other items, so people had Ration Books with coupons in them, which meant that you could only get a limited amount of the things you needed, on a regular basis. Some men used to put tea into their pipes and smoke it as tobacco was scarce. Many shops had very empty shelves. The youth of today would have no real idea as to what people had to endure back then.

"Spindle Shanks" told me that she remembered going with her mother to a town about four miles away from her village to get a bag of flour for making bread. They brought a donkey who was able to walk on a narrow pathway to town. All one could see were high walls of snow piled up on both sides and they were threatening. The bag of flour was purchased, put up on the donkey's back and then held there as the donkey moved along, on the homeward journey. About a mile from home, the bag of flour fell off the donkey's back down on the frozen snow. With effort, the bag was hoisted back up again and eventually reached base, lucky in that they had their own supply. Foodstuffs were scarce at that time and there were no luxuries.

Fuel was also scarce but country people were lucky in that they had a supply of turf and maybe timber to keep them warm. The houses were often freezing cold then as there was no such thing as central heating, in many cases.

As the freezing continued, farmers were running out of fodder for the cattle. The hay they had had to be rationed and instead of cutting the hay with a hay knife, they resorted to just pulling a bit of hay out with their hands, so as to use less of it.

In the Forties in rural Ireland there was no electricity which meant that people had to rely on paraffin oil lamps and candles for light. Needless to say, the light from these was very poor and it is a miracle tha people then did not all go blind, trying to read in the dim light.

When people died there was a problem. They could not be buried for some time because the earth was frozen to a great depth. This was particularly true in the early stages of the freeze-up, when transport was also out of action.

The positive aspect of the Winter wonderland was that it gave the children much time off school and they enjoyed pelting snowballs at one another, making snowmen and snowwomen, sliding and skating on the ice, tobogganing, riding on sledges and so on.

The lakes were frozen thick and they became playgrounds as well. People danced on them, bands played music on them and some even drove cars across them. It was all so unreal.

While the young enjoyed the ice and snow, it was very difficult for the elderly folk. They were very confined indoors and in those days there was no television and only an odd household had a radio. They were simple times but people managed to survive.

The thaw came in late March and into April but there was still snow in the fields in May and in some places there were big blocks of snow there in June.

Decades have passed since that blizzard and there has not been any repeat of it, thank God. Let's hope it never returns to our water-washed shores. If it happened today, I think we would be better able to cope with it, as the country has advanced in many ways compared to 1947. It must be said that because we do not usually get much snow in Ireland, we are never that prepared for it, when it comes our way.

I am grateful to our dear "Spindle Shanks" for her memories of the big freeze and perhaps, at least some of the readers of this account, may be prompted to relive it, once again.

Big Snow of 1947

Cracker and Candy – The Brimstone Two

I was told recently about two people who live down there in Brimstone. They are brother and sister, in their Seventies. The locals call them "The Brimstone Two".

Their sole occupation is taking other people apart and nothing is barred. The locals are all afraid of them because they dread coming under their scrutiny and they try to avoid contact with them, as much as possible. I visited The Brimstone Two last week as I wanted to get some idea as to how they operate. They were very welcoming and also curious to know what brought me to the village.

I did not tell them that I had come to study their form but that I heard they were very good at relating facts about people that others might not know.

They seemed to accept what I said and then offered me coffee and a scone. The brother, Cracker began the conversation about a member of a family in another village called Brickland who had just got married for the fifth time. He was one of the Farten family in which there were seven in total. His name was Jack Pat Thomas. He was the eldest of the clutch. He was a cattle dealer, of sorts.

Cracker described him as being rough, tough and nasty with no interest in anything or anyone but women. Signs were on him, four wives died under his rulership. No one put manners on him when he was a youngster growing up. The sister, Candy nodded the head and gave her full approval to Cracker's comments.

Next moment, she started up and had a go at twin sisters in the same family. They were like two artificial dolls with fancy clothes and jewellery and loaded with make-up. That was Jerky and Jenny. No wonder they got jobs in the beauty business. You could not say much good about the pair. They did not have much shape or good looks. In fact, they always had sour pusses on them and they would cut you dead if you criticised them to their faces.

What would you expect seeing that they came from that wretched place called Brickland. Some real villains came out of that hole. My God protect us all from the likes of those.

Cracker seconded her remarks and picked up where she left off. He launched into the male twins in the family. They were called Honk and Tonk. Though they were supposed to be twins they were very unlike, in ways. Honk became a drug dealer and made massive amounts of money but squandered it all on living the high life, travelling the world and staying in five star hotels. He was as mean as dirt and never gave a penny to support any cause, not that anyone would want his illegally earned money. He had ways of avoiding the Law.

Tonk was never fond of work. He liked to idle and mess around and when he got bored doing nothing he went off to Thailand and married some weird lady there. They both joined a big circus.

He was the stuntman and she was supporting him, showing herself off, in fancy uniforms. They were both bad yokes because they were into all kinds of trickery. No one would want to see either of them ever again, back in Brickland or in any other place .

As soon as Cracker finished his piece, Candy applauded, pulled out her hankie and cleared her nose before continuing her description of another member of the Fartens. This time it was "The Tank", a real big lady, twenty two stone in weight. The roads around Brickland were never built for the likes of her. They are far too narrow and she could get stuck between the ditches along the sides. The pressure could spark off a considerable tremor.

She never raised her wings, a stay- at-home bird and she managed to hold on to the little farm the family had. The locals gave her a nickname that she detested. Every time she heard it, she would stamp on the ground and fly off the handle, cursing and swearing. She had a fierce tongue when agitated, and a quick temper.

One day she met a tiny little man on the road called Flat Foot and he made some remark about her weight, without thinking. Next thing she drew out and gave him an unmerciful belt across the face and floored him. She then gave him an awful kick in the stomach with her heavy boots and marched off leaving the poor little man, stretched on the ground and crying for help. She was an awkward piece of goods if her feathers were ruffled and she could recite more than the Litany of Loreto.

She never got anyone to put a ring on her finger, so she lived in single blessedness, admiring the plants and the trees around her residence. She drank brandy, privately, but when she exited her abode, she gave the game away because her face had lighted up and she was as red as a turkey cock.

She kept bee-hives in the garden and one day they attacked her when she opened up a hive and nearly stung her to death. Only for a neighbouring man, Ratchet came and rescued her by driving the bees back with smoking fuel in a bucket. She was sore, red and blistered for a long time after that. She never spoke of bees after that. It was always "The Bitches".

The Clocker McNamara remarked that it was a pity that some sportsman or sportswoman did not discover her as she would make a great heavy-weight boxer or wrestler because she had the muscle and the build for that. Stonewall Jackson fully agreed that she was very solid on the ground and almost immovable once she put her two feet on terra firma.

As soon as Candy dried up, Cracker was in, in a shot and called for a round of applause for her.

He then got going on The Bull, a Farten family member who set himself up in a very wild place beside a big lake because he loved boats and fishing and all things water. The area was called Snipetown which gives some indication of the nature of the land there, only fit for wildlife. He was a pig farmer and that suited him well, as he loved to eat any amount of fat salty bacon.

The Bull was not the usual specimen of human that walks around these parts or any others. He was six feet and eight inches in height with a head of hair resembling an Amazonian forest in the middle of Summer. There must have been some fauna in it and maybe even a bit of flora too. No barber ever touched it.

He was extremely skinny, of the knitting needle type but he had very big feet, so big that the shoe shops never had a shoe to fit him. He used to get his shoes via an old auntie that he had in Philadelphia by the name of Blinkers. She always had trouble with her bad eyes, but the poor thing was generous.

When The Bull walked he resembled the Leaning Tower of Pisa, going in one direction, straying away from the perpendicular. He walked with the feet always turned out, as if the left foot was not on terms with the right one, poles apart, as they say. He had a very noticeable limp also and he was often like a boat on the water, swaying one way and then another. They say that he often had Sea Sickness even when on dry land.

He was called "The Bull" because of his strength. He was able to bend pieces of strong steel with his hands and lift weights of all sizes and shapes.

One of his pastimes which was fishing on the lake near his home, ended his life abruptly. He was out on the water one very wintery evening and the wind was high. The boat capsized and he fell into the water. He sank quickly and was drowned. No one noticed that he was not around for about a week which was sad.

Cracker ended on this note and Candy stood up to get more refreshments but I said that I was in a hurry as I was flying to Hong Kong in the morning. She took no notice of what I said and proceeded to make tea and arrived back with it plus some apple tart.

Candy then insisted on me hearing one other bit of news before I made my getaway. She opened up and tore into a villager called locally Frosty as she had a very austere look about her. She said that if you met her, you would think you were back in the time of the Great Famine. She did a very bad job of rearing her family and they all ended up in some kind of misfortune. The eldest guy, Mopsie, shot two youngsters down in Multylack, all on account of a disagreement. He was locked up for twelve years. The youngest daughter, Bonkers – well christened – had two children by different fathers and they were adopted by a couple down in Jinksland. She was really something, A son called Clogs emigrated to Thailand and lost his life in a train crash. She could go on for the rest of the night but I was in a hurry and had to leave their company.

I told the pair that I enjoyed their chat very much and then we shook hands and I sped off in my twenty year old banger, hoping that it would keep going until I got home. Fortunately, it obliged, on this occasion.

Sometime later I happened to be at Mass in the church of all Saints in the parish of Bradachbeg and the priest celebrating the Mass was Fr. Ricky Random. He was a young handsome man with a great sense of humour but he was also well able to give advice to his people in order to keep them from straying into bad ways.

I thought that his Homily on the day was well worth delivering but I am not able to do justice to what he said. Suffice it to say that I will give a brief summary of what he said. He began with a little story by way of introduction.

He began his real message by saying that some people have two faces, one when they are out in public and it is grand and pleasing to all. Then, when they get into close range with a few people either at home or out in a pub or such place, they launch an attack on certain individuals or families. They put on a different face then and they show up their critical and nasty side, often with a certain amount of hatred or jealousy. They need to quit this carry on.

Those people are quick to see the faults and failings in others but totally disregard their own faults and shortcomings. They can see the beam in their neighbours' eye but not the plank in their own. How true that is.

I could not help thinking of Cracker and Candy and I hope they were there to get the message.

Frankie the Yankee – An Emigrant Returns

Down there in the village of Pollnagower lives *Frankie the Yankee*. That's what everyone around calls him, because though he was born and reared in the above village, he spent about forty years in Chicago and returned home with a considerable nest-egg, a big accumulation of dollars. His line of work in the States was Real Estate.

Frankie has taken back to Ireland many American ideas and peculiarities, but despite that, he has fitted in well with the Pollnagower ways of doing things or not doing them at all, as the case may be.

His worse trait is his temper which is hot, quick and explosive. I hear that he did not take that from the side of the road. His father before him could set the place on fire with his temper, and God protect anyone that may have ignited the said feature. Frankie has a sharp tongue, a nasty vocabulary and a threatening look in his big red eyes.

Recently Slinker happened to cross his path because his donkeys broke into his vegetable plot and made complete praiseach of everything in it. He confronted Slinker and gave him an unmerciful telling off. Sparks flew and so did Slinker. I believe no prayers were uttered at all that day. Frankie told the culprit that if this ever happened again he would blow his head off and break every bone in his body, in several parts. Any feeling of neighbourliness that existed between the pair, prior to this incident, had by now evaporated.

He has a black cover on one of his eyes but he can see far too much with the other eye. The cover gives him a kind of tough look.

Slinker was scared and went into a bit of a shiver as he reflected on his future. He at once jumped up on his thirty year old tractor with the forklift and hit for the local Co-Op Store, purchased a consignment of stakes and barbed wire and on his return, did a fine fencing job along the dividing line or mearing between his own land and that of Frankie. The job done, a life was spared.

Trespassing was always an awful problem in rural areas and mearing fences and the like were also very problematic, if they were not well maintained. Many fights took place over transgressions and there were cases even of loss of life, not to mention the bad feelings that lasted for years, between neighbouring families. Rights of way were another great headache and Solomon himself could not resolve some of the cases that arose. Love your neighbour as yourself did not seem to enter the picture at all, despite the fact that all parties claimed to be Christians.

To describe Frankie physically is challenging. He has been compared to many different features. A journalist who came to the area last year said that Frankie resembled the Eiffel Tower, narrow at the top and magnificently wide at the bottom. Another visitor to the village said that he was like a badly designed vehicle at the rear and like a leaning tower at the front. He is nearly seven feet tall and when out and about is buffeted by the wind.

When in his presence, a straight face is recommended, for safety. An outburst of laughter would give rise to a terminal situation for the culprit.

When he goes to the local tavern, he swings into Pub Mode. This is when he starts up conversation with anyone at all and in no time, he reminds the one he is chatting up that he left the house in a hurry, being distracted by his noisy barking security dog, and that he forgot to bring his wallet. This excuse goes down like lead but the generosity of the other person wins through and Frankie has a big frothy pint planked down in front of him, free gratis and for nothing. In spite of all his wealth, he is as mean as hell, a real scrounger. Frankie has tried this stunt many times so the local guys decided to teach him a lesson.

One of the lads in the pub engaged Frankie with a chat about a musical instrument which he got him to try out as he was fond of music. While this was going on, another fellow got a pint of porter at the counter and then dropped a very powerful laxative into it. He left it in front of Frankie and said that it was on the house. There was a look of joy about the man's face. His eyes lit up. After all, it was a free pint.

As he was well oiled at the time, he did not notice any difference in the liquid. In a split second, after draining the glass, an urgency set in. There was a mad dash from the bar to the nearest toilet, and there were obstacles in the way which delayed Frankie's flight. Unfortunately, he did not make the desired destination in time. Disaster struck and it was expected, in some quarters.

There was no need for one for the road on this occasion. The pub owner, I heard, gave Frankie a change of clothing but the lads said that there was an odour in the air, not one you would associate with roses or any other bloom that you may have in your garden.

Frankie loves horses and places bets on them, every day, in the local Bookmaker's Shop. He rarely wins anything as he is quite poor on the research side of the horses' forms. His method of selecting the horses he wishes to place a bet on is not very scientific. He leaves the open racing page of the newspaper down, flat on the kitchen table and then closes his eyes. He simply sticks a pin into the horses' names and on opening his eyes again, he writes down the names on a slip of paper for the bookie.

That is Frankie's way of doing business. He has, however, an interesting addendum to this. He has a great devotion to St. Anthony of Padua and in his abode he has a large statue of the saint on a mantelpiece. The statue is hollow on the inside and Frankie rolls up his list of horses and pushes it up into the statue for good luck. Then he retrieves it again, and off he goes to the bookie's shop, spiritually armed. Smart work, Frankie!

One other thing! Frankie believes that you have a better chance of winning if the horses you back have funny names. One day I asked him to give me a short list of these, just for fun. He suddenly opened up and spat them out at me, with haste.

The ones I managed to catch were: One for the Road; Bitchy Bob; Trip Switch; Laughing Larry; Rainbow; Silly Sally; Billy's Beano; Earthquake; Hurricane; Lollipop; Mr. Super and many more. I placed my bets on some of them but I am still waiting for a windfall. I am afraid that Frankie's wisdom is somewhat suspect, in my estimation.

As well as backing horses, he has another fad that he took home with him from North America. Every Friday he drives to Connemara to carry out some panning for gold in the lively glistening waters of the rivers and streams. He seriously believes that he will find gold there and as regards the mountains, he says they contain gold also.

It is hard to understand why he would waste his time in this way, as he does not need any gold for he is loaded already. A local man, Pat the Plank told him recently to cop himself on. He told him that the only gold in those parts is Fools' Gold and it has no value at all. He should drive home and have a slug of whiskey.

Frankie did not like his remark and responded: *You should put a bit of tape on your big gob and mind your own business. I am a man of considerable intelligence and I know my onions. Good day to you, Sir!*

Dick the Trick and Francie – The Male Dudes

In the tiny village of Crubeen South is where the two bachelor brothers of doubtful fame reside. They are referred to locally as *The Lads.* They are in their Fifties but still have thoughts of marriage on the brain, not that they need women in the house at all as they now have good experience in household chores. The elder brother is called *Dick the Trick* by the villagers and the younger lad, Francie the Fatso. Their surname is Rickety but it is seldom used.

The Chef among them is Dick and he boasts long and loudly about his expertise with cuisine. He expounds on numerous dishes, from soups to meat, fish, potatoes and even pasta. He has quite an array of saucepans and pots and an expensive oven, with warning lights that kick up a racket if anything goes wrong. He bought it once when he was in Thailand, on a holiday.

I tasted some of his cooking and to be honest I felt that the hygiene was not great and he pays little attention to temperatures. He ignores the sell by date on things he buys, but he has one strong point. It is his fine garden of vegetables which he uses, on a regular basis. He is addicted to onions and rhubarb and speaks eloquently on the nutritional value of leeks and broccoli. He certainly looks well himself, despite my concerns about his cooking.

The Fatso does all the washing up and usually creates a pool of water on the floor. Sometimes he does a spot of cooking. He has just one dish that he dispenses when in the mood. It is, as he says, a Pudding, but beyond that, it could be anything at all. The recipe for this is not documented. I have not sampled this stuff myself but a neighbour I know has eaten this luxury and he ended up by being sick for a month after indulging in it. He didn't actually call it Pudding. He gave it another name – Nuclear Poison.

The Fatso is a bit simple, not quite the full shilling, a bit half-baked and dangerous also, at times. One day he took an axe and went out into the garden to cut down a shrub. The dog Tweezer followed him and made a big fuss barking. He turned around in a rage, swung the axe and beheaded the dog, on the spot.

The pair do most things together. They live in a thatched cottage and every year it has to get a fresh coat of thatch in order to maintain the structure, in good condition. The Trick thatches the front roof and The Fatso does the back.

They have a real old rusty banger of a car, long overdue in the scrap yard, away beyond its sell by date. It belongs to another age but the funny thing about it is that it moves. The Fatso says that it has a powerful engine and that the proof of his statement is the mountain of black smoke that comes out of the exhaust. If you believe that, you will believe anything. Another proof, he says, is the great amount of oil it burns even on a spin down the road. His brain must be on a coffee break.

Winking Willie down the road is monitoring this vehicle. He says that the only way it could ever pass an NCT would be for the pair to bribe the tester or present him with a crate of high-class whiskey or such like. They might even drug the man and on waking, they would have eloped with the wreck.

When making a journey, The Trick drives to the predetermined destination and then The Fatso drives on the way back. This can be described as a division of labour.

Despite their age, they include in their schedule, social events, including ballroom dancing. Their legs were never designed for such manouvres and one night when The Fatso was dancing with a big heavy lady, his awkward boots landed on top of her toes which left her almost disabled for the rest of her life. Luckily, she was able to take the floor again after twelve months. The Fatso didn't even say he was sorry to the lady. He crossly told her to keep her big fat feet to herself in future.

The thinking behind their attendance at social events was to provide an opportunity to meet a suitable prospective marriage partner. May God protect the poor girls that might be so daft as to take up their offers. You know, in spite of everything, they fancy themselves. You could call it the Crubeen Dream!

The Fatso is into many activities, in his own tin pot way. He does the Euromillions, not to mention the dogs. He also plays Bingo but has never won anything. He says that if he keeps on losing, he will probably commit suicide. He can down a pint as good as the next but one pint is all it takes to turn him on. Then he becomes completely mental and loses the bit of a mind that he has. He usually turns to singing and he gives a blast of *Glory, Glory, Alleluia – when the saints go marching in.*

You may be wondering why Dick is known as The Trick. Well, I can fill you in on this, by way of a few examples.

Down the village there was an old man in his Eighties and he had cattle on his small farm. He wanted to sell them but did not know what they were worth.

The Trick got wind of this and sent a con-man called The Mule to value the cattle, pretending that he was an auctioneer from the local Mart. He valued the cattle at about one third of what their real value was.

He got a backhand from The Trick for his work and he then moved in and bought the cattle, took them to the Mart and got a huge price for them there as they were excellent cattle. No wonder The Trick went on whiskey and soda for a week after.

On another occasion The Trick went to a village ten miles away from Crubeen and it was then close to Christmas. He called to a farm and posed as an official from the Department of Agriculture. He said that there was a serious outbreak of fowl disease and that he had come to take away all the Christmas turkeys for slaughter.

By arrangement, the Con-Man arrived, with a false face and loaded up the turkeys on his trailer. Fine birds they were and well fed all year. Then, off the pair went as a great shower of hailstones fell from the heavens.

The Con-Man, once again got his pay-off and The Trick sold the turkeys to a butcher he knew in another village called Slosh. He had a money-filled Christmas that year, the blackguard.

The Trick was also reputed to have stolen tools, cars and tractors and sold them off to clients, in remote parts. He was a cool, calculated operator who always covered his tracks. It can be said that he was Crubeen's version of Al Capone, minus Alcatraz.

Haytime as it Used to Be

I was down in the village of Slosheen recently and I called in to have a chat with an old man I know for many years. He is "The Badger" Flynn and he is now in his nineties.

He is a retired farmer and he likes to reflect on the old ways of farming, of which he had great experience. He broke into talking to me about haymaking as it used to be done when he was young and indeed as it was done, much later on as well.

In pre-mechanisation days, cutting the meadows was quite laborious. The meadows had to be cut by men armed with a good scythe and a scythe-stone for sharpening the blade of the scythe when it got blunt. Experienced mowers were able to cut the grass with precision.

While this work was going on the men were sustained with good food and there was usually a big jar of porter brought on site for extra nourishment. It was a task that took some time as it was a slow process, especially if the crop was heavy.

As time went on, the mowing machine came into being which was a great step forward. The machine was drawn by a team of horses, two good animals who could work together. The farmer then could sit up on a seat at the back of the machine, like a king on his throne, take the reins in his hands and drive the horses forward.

As a youth, I often walked behind the machine, with rake in hand as a kind of assistant to the man on the seat. My role was to remove any grass that might get caught in the blade or elsewhere, so that the work could continue. It was a tiring job, walking around and around a big field all day. The perks were few and far between but one did have some food and drink. This was a task that should have a shoe allowance attached.

In doing the rounds, one had time to admire all the lovely wild grasses and colourful flowers. Frogs were leaping, hither and thither, some of them disabled, after getting caught in the blade of the machine. Birds too, rose up out of the meadows and created their own music. You could never forget the scent of the newly cut grass and it was even better later on, when it dried and became hay.

In due course, the mowing machine and the team of horses gave way to the tractor and its attached mower and it too was used for bringing the cocks of hay into the haggard with a forklift.

Many other new machines came on the market, as time went on, such as hay-tedders, silage-makers and balers. The machinery brought an end to the old manual way of haymaking and that meant less labour on all fronts.

The farmer was always watching the weather and would not venture out to cut grass until there were signs of a good dry spell. Haymaking is one operation for which fine weather is necessary and if a year happened to be very wet, then the quality of the hay was never great.

When the grass was cut for a day or two, the swades of grass were turned over to assist drying before it was shaken out, using forks. That was to spread the grass evenly over the ground to enable it to dry. When dry it would be made into little cocks, known as Foot Cocks. They were called by that name because they were formed by using a rake and help from the left or right foot.

The next chore was to gather the foot cocks into certain locations and they were then used to build the big cocks of hay and there might be twenty five or thirty of these in a field. The entire area had then to be raked, manually which gave a lovely clean look to the meadow.

All the cocks had to be roped in order to prevent the wind from knocking them down or blowing the hay around the field. It took two people to make the ropes from the hay. One person took a piece of hay and put it around a bit of a stick and then fed the hay into the rope while the other person twisted the rope by turning the stick in his or her hand.

About a week or so later, the cocks were taken in from the fields to the haggard and either put indoors in a shed or built into ricks or large cocks in the garden near the house. The way in which they were taken in from the fields entailed putting chains around and under the cocks and then they were pulled by a horse, pony or donkey into the haggard. Sometimes, the chains would be pulled through the hay and the cock would be left behind.

Of course, machinery is expensive to buy and not all farmers were able to purchase some of the new equipment. Some small farms would not justify the outlay so, they used to hire the machines which proved far more economic for them. This is very much the case where baling and silage-making are concerned.

I was very happy to get such information and memories from "The Badger" Flynn who had first-hand experience with all the old operations for haymaking, from cuttings with a scythe to mowing the grass with a tractor.

My own memories of meadows in Summer-time are of the wind agitating the meadow grass like the tides on the ocean, the scents of newly cut grass, the wild flowers, birds singing, notably the cuckoo and the exhilarating fresh air.

These are things that have remained in my mind's eye, down the years and in a way, they remind me of Wordsworth's poem – *The Daffodils.* For him, like me, the daffodils flashed upon his inward eye and gave him a happy feeling in his solitude.

In remote areas of the country, one can still see the old-fashioned haymaking going on, presumably due to a lack of money or resources. It could also be due to the farms being very small and they would not warrant a big outlay for machinery.

One last remark! Be sure to make the hay while the sun shines. If you do, the quality will be good and the animals that you feed it to, will know the difference. They will eat it, with relish.

Willie the Wig – Commentator

There is a local radio station in the townland of Dickeenmore and it is very popular in the area and beyond. It is well equipped and it has two well qualified technicians to look after it, when on air.

The technicians are twins and the people there call them by their nickname which is Stilts because they are extremely tall and as lanky as a telegraph pole. As Imelda the Twitch remarked: *The temperature up there at their skulls is away lower than that down at their big toes.*

The radio station boss is Fat Freddy, well educated, according to some know-alls, and he shows it when on air with his daily programme *Tit Bits and More.*

The best known member of the station staff is the man with the golden voice who does the commentaries on the horse races down in the local racecourse. He is Willie the Wig and he backs horses himself, every day, and enjoys a few pints every evening.

He lives in a two storey thatched house which looks very funny to me as I would be more accustomed to seeing one storey thatched cottages. That's the way it is and at least the Wig can have a good view of the racecourse from the upper storey. Silly Cissie calls him The Pope as he dresses up ceremoniously and she says he might even give *An Urbi et Orbi* from the top storey. If push came to shove, he could manage a race commentary from there if he had his binoculars.

He is an expert on the horses' form, winnings and losings as he does his research in such a way as to have a good chance of winning something and getting a bit back from the bookie. The locals have him tortured looking for tips but as Leaping Lizzie put it: *He is a downright villain as he keeps all the best tips to himself, the scrounger. I wouldn't give him a mouthful of anything even if he were dying from the thirst.*

Curious to listen in to one of his race commentaries, I turned on the local radio station one day and I must say that his voice is good and clear and he certainly knows his horses. I recorded his performance and it is a fine example of his style. In due course, you can read the words of his race description and I hope you enjoy it.

In the meantime, I want to let you in on a top secret, known only to the inner circle of Willie's friends. With them, he opens up and gives insights into his eventful life. He was kind of married five times and after the fifth wife died, he ran out of steam and returned to the single state, a state in which he is in now.

His first wife, known to him as Lantern didn't shed much light, it seems because she left him after three years and then Fairy came along, fancy as hell, but no good for a day in the bog. She lasted five years. They had words so the bird took flight and later it was learned that she joined an order of Nuns. No one knows where she actually went.

Wife number three was a big awkward blonde with a fierce appetite. Her name was Sparkler. The barrel Brennan remarked about her. He said that she was very wooden and giggly and needed a great deal of parking space. Willie couldn't handle her at all so he gave her a P45, but not before sparks flew in all directions. Her tenure of office was just a year and a half.

When wife four arrived, Honeysuckle, that is, all could see that she was a good and wise woman with common sense to give away. She kept The Wig on the straight and narrow but he was never seen practising anything in the religious line. He certainly was not a Catholic. The Duck Sweeney believes that he was an agnostic, searching for the truth. So far, it seems to have eluded him. Puncher McGurrin thinks that he is now an out and out atheist. He could be right.

The fifth and last wife of Willie the Wig was Blusher, a big heavy tank of a woman, a real strong agricultural type of female. As Frisky Frank put it: *If she got stuck in a drain, it would take a good tractor to move her and pull her out . She lasted for eighteen years but her obesity killed her at the heel of the hunt. The locals said that she always had a wild look and you would feel threatened in her company. She would blast you out of it, as quickly as you could say Jack Robinson.*

The Funny Man in the area, Shivers was asked did he know what happened to Wig's fifth wife. He smiled and said: *My guess is as good as anyone else's, because Willie did not divulge a thing relevant to her. I would say that she had some kind of plumbing trouble, and that's it.*

It is now time to let you read Willie the Wig's Commentary that I promised you –

> *And they are off to a good start with Tickle Me Stiff taking the lead, followed closely by Undercoat, Goggle Box and Crazy Biddy. Then a short distance behind comes Drunken Dick, Sidestep, Silly Billy and Monkey Man. They are travelling at a rocket pace over this two mile circuit.*
>
> *Crazy Biddy has now taken up the running and is out in front chased by Goggle Box, Undercoat and Tickle Me Stiff.*
>
> *The back group is quickening pace now and is putting pressure on the leaders. Drunken Dick is moving up with Silly Billy to offer a challenge.*
>
> *Sidestep has just now unsaddled the jockey. He is on the ground and now Monkey Man has fallen. Goggle Box and Undercoat have dropped back but Tickle Me stiff is improving on the outside. He is going well.*
>
> *Here comes Drunken Dick, closing the gap and behind him is Silly Billy. Tickle Me Stiff now takes the lead and the pace is faster again. Drunken Dick is now pushing forward with great gusto and takes the lead from Tickle Me Stiff. Silly Billy has moves up into third place with a furlong to go, it looks like the latter three.*
>
> *Goggle box is now positioned in fourth place and looks determined. Into*

the straight and Silly Billy makes a break for the winning post, chasing victory, gaining a few lengths on Drunken Dick. He hangs on to win from Drunken Dick with Tickle Me Stiff in third place.

I hear that Goggle Box who fell awkwardly in the race, is being put down as he broke a leg. The jockeys on Sidestep and Monkey Man escaped injury.

The prices at the bookies were as follows:

1. *Silly Billy – 12/1;*
2. *Drunken Dick – Favourite -2/1;*
3. *Tickle Me Stiff – 7/1.*

Willie has more strings to his bow than commentating. He is a great dancer and he gives performances in the local halls, from time to time, for a fee. He does not believe in doing things for nothing. He says that people have no respect for freebies, so put a fee on, and they respect the event, much better. That's his view.

I spent some quality time in Dickeenmore and learned a great deal about its residents. It has many colourful characters and they are people of wit. If you have a good sense of humour, come to this place. If not, it might be better for you to go elsewhere. I hope you have got the message. You have been warned.

Last week I happened to meet Mal Goldenfoot and he is a mad racing man. He attends all the local race meetings and backs horses, in a big way. He has won some big amounts of money but he knows his horses and jockeys, inside out. He is a good man to ask for a tip, when he is in the right mood.

He began talking about Willie the Wig and complimented him on his work. He stressed the importance of good commentators. They can make a race exciting, especially when you are listening in, on radio. When you have placed bets, you want to hear the race exactly as it is happening.

As I was talking to a racing man, I had to agree with him. As he left me, he was heading off to one of his bet-placing sessions. I hope he wins something because backing horses is a dodgy business, most times, but you can be lucky, now and again.

Remembering the Travelling People of Old

I had a bit of spare time recently so I decided to take a trip, in my less than luxurious car, to a place called Portachmore. That comes from the Gaelic and it means the Big Bog. It is very apt as a name because there are acres and acres of bogland there.

My mission there was to meet a lady who had a great name for remembering the olden times and all that went with them. The local people call her Jelly because when she starts talking she always goes into a shiver and keeps on shaking while she is telling her tales. She does not have any stammer and she speaks clearly and distinctly. Her face has a wrinkle for every day in the year but the wrinkles suit her.

She was pleased to meet me and I found her willing to talk to me about anything I liked. I said that I would like her to tell me something about the Travelling People she knew when she was young and she agreed to oblige me.

She remembered the time she was going to Primary School away back in the 1940's. She had to walk to school and often carried sods of turf for the fire in school under her arm. There was no such thing then as central heating. The fire was needed also for heating the kids' bottles of milk, cocoa or tea and often there were explosions as the heat used to pop the corks or even break the bottles, if the fire was too good. It was like a smaller version of Hiroshima.

On rare occasions, she might have a big old – fashioned bicycle which she rode to school. She had a choice of two routes to school, a long route, following the main road or a shortcut which was a narrow boreen. It was lovely and quiet, with little or no traffic on it, day or night. There were a few small houses along it, but not all of them were close to the boreen.

Because of its quietness and privacy, the travelling people used to come and set up their camps or tents along the sides of this little road. They were simple structures consisting of canvass spread on top of a framework of bamboo or other type of rods, with a part that could be opened or closed as required. That was to facilitate entry and exiting.

On her way to school in the morning she had a close-up view of all the action. The travellers were always up early and there was usually a big fire burning near the camp, the materials having come from the farmers in the vicinity. They would mainly be sods of turf, sticks and brambles from the wild vegetation. The fire was very inviting on a cold frosty morning.

The father and mother of the family would be seated on the ground, beside the fire, where there might be a kettle or a saucepan boiling on top of the flames. Very young kids could be seen running around the camp outside and not a stitch of clothes on them. They seemed to be completely oblivious to the cold. The fire was the only thing they had for cooking whatever food they ate.

Close to the encampment there was a horse or two eating a bit of hay and looking somewhat untidy and in need of grooming. Horse manure was evident and it was plentiful. There was also a cart parked on the roadside, with the shafts pointing upwards and pieces of harness nearby. This was their version of the rich man's Mercedes.

The father of this family was known as Ginger and the wife was referred to as Pepper. They had ten in family, six girls and four boys. They all attended the local Primary School and it was nice to see them mixing with the rest of the children and they seemed to get on well together. Jelly said that this particular family was well liked in the area by all the people. They were law-abiding and did not get into any trouble, either with the people or the Gardaí.

On the return journey from school Jelly used to get another view of traveller activity. Some of the youngsters would be cooking food or washing dishes, while the father, Ginger and his sons would be making items out of tin such as saucepans, tin cans, little mugs and much more. They looked content and happy to be busy as they would be able to sell the products to the locals and at the fairs and get a bit of money for them.

The mother, Pepper must have been busy, too, because the ditches were covered with colourful items of clothing, newly washed. Some items were hanging from pieces of twine or rope attached to branches of the trees. There was plenty of evidence of work in progress and all the while, they were communicating in a language of their own so that no one could know what they were saying.

This and other traveller families in those times were well behaved, respected and had a very good relationship with the local people. They often called around to the houses and the women used to give them a dinner, a drink and other refreshments. The men used to give them turf for the fire and hay for the horses. They were always grateful for the generosity and even recited a prayer or a blessing for the donor.

The travellers of old were very religious or as some people thought, superstitious. They went to Church regularly and especially to Mass. They frequented places of Pilgrimage and seemed to have a particular devotion to the Blessed Virgin Mary.

The young girls used to attend, smartly dressed or maybe only half-dressed and parade a bit, in order to attract the attention of the young men, with a view to marriage. The travellers always married young and had big families.

It is an established fact that people who live a deprived and impoverished life, have a very high fertility rate. This is borne out by the huge populations in the Third World countries.

Where dress was concerned, the older traveller women wore long skirts of strong material and big heavy shawls, while the menfolk also dressed in good robust jackets and trousers, all meant, I suppose, to cope with their hard, austere lives.

Footwear was usually sturdy and strong on both male and female travellers. The younger members dressed more lightly and were more fashion conscious, even back then.

The travellers of old looked healthy but many had poor health, inside. Many of them died much younger than the settled population, due to their difficult living conditions. Over-exposure to the elements did not help their physical wellbeing. When any of them died, they had particular practices which they rigidly implemented.

When one looked into their faces, it was easy to see that they had come through hardship and deprivation. Jelly often felt that any settled person could have been born into a traveller family, depending on who one's parents were. A sobering thought, no doubt.

It is heartening to see the progress travelling people have made in recent times. They have left the roadside camps behind and have fancy caravans, vehicles, possessions, better halting sites, even houses, better schooling and education, employment and ways of making a living as traders. There are signs of prosperity which can only be for the better. They also have spokespeople who can articulate their needs and aspirations and stand up for them on radio and television.

Jelly was emphatic that the old days and the old ways would not be returning and that is good news for the travelling community which is now gaining in confidence and understanding the benefits that come from living a better kind of life than their ancestors. The old inferiority feeling is waning and a new dawn is gradually awakening.

Down the years the powers that be did not cover themselves in glory when one looks at the conditions travellers had to live in. No ordinary person would have tolerated that, but anything that was done for them was very disjointed and primitive. They were often just moved on, from place to place. Red tape and soft chat took the place of real action on the ground and the long finger approach was common.

There is still an attitude problem. Many settled people have very negative views regarding travellers. They may be justified, in some cases, where travellers let themselves down by their behaviour, so they need to change their ways also. Other travellers gain respect from the public when they behave properly. It will take more time for full integration.

Crappy and Goggles of Pisheen West

When Pontius and Philo passed away down in the village of Pisheen West, the only members of the family at home were two sons, Crappy and Goggles. The rest of the family had taken flight to America and apparently, had good jobs there.

No Will had been made by Pontius and Philo so the house and farm and other assets were open to all family members to claim their share. It was unlikely that the American members would be interested in the estate at all as they were well off and settled over there. They would have sentimental and emotional ties with home, but no more than that. The two lads at home were looking at each other, anxious to make some sort of decision about themselves and the farm.

They contacted a solicitor and he advised them to get the family members in America to sign off their interests in the home place. He then wrote to all of them and they were agreeable to sign the necessary documents. They were no way awkward or difficult. This brought great relief to Crappy and Goggles.

That much decided, it was then a question of a decision between the two boys themselves. They could both live on the farm and share everything or one could opt out and leave the house and farm to the other. The one opting to remain, could offer some compensation to the one leaving.

They deliberated long and hard on the options. They decided that it would be hard for two people to make a good living on a small farm, especially if they married and had families to keep.

Crappy, aged twenty five, was the one with the keenest interest in the land and farming whereas Goggles who was twenty two, was more of what you might call, a gentleman farmer who didn't like dirtying his hands. He had a much greater interest in acting and singing. At the heel of the hunt, he decided to pack his bag and go to London in search of work and he went, a week later.

A close-up look at Goggles is worthwhile because he was unique in ways. He was regarded as a bit mad by some and definitely wild by many. He loved all things fast such as posh cars, racing bikes, horses, motorbikes and much more. He was terribly stylish and well-groomed and could even put on a fancy accent. You would think that he was more like a city Slicker than a product of Pisheen West. He always had a flashy watch and a hairstyle to catch anyone's eye. It was bare at the sides with tall spikes of hair standing erect on top of his head resembling factory chimneys in an industrial area. They always caught the wind and, of course, attracted attention.

Goggles could be as daft as hell at times like the day he jumped into the local freezing river with all his clothes on, or the night he dismantled the donkey cart that was in the farmyard and then brought it into the kitchen, bit by bit, and reassembled it there, before yoking up their donkey to it, tying him to an armchair and leaving him to enjoy a big bundle of hay for his nourishment. He was trying to impress his brother but he was no way impressed by his prank.

When he got up on his motorbike, it was a very dangerous time because he usually went mad down the road, making an awful noise as the silencer was defective. He always wore goggles and that is how he got his nickname. A local lady, Julia Mucker described him as a raving luper that should not be let out at all without a restrainer.

Goggles found himself a job in London, in a theatre there. He fancied himself as an actor and he was a very good singer, despite his rather silly nature and behaviour. He got parts in big shows such as *The Phantom of the Opera, Miss Saigon* and many other shows of note in the West End.

One night he was in a nightclub and there was a cabaret show on the programme, billed for 11.00 p.m. He waited on for it and in it was a group of twelve dancers and a leading lady. They were all tall, slim and scantily clad, with big branches of feathers on their heads and also at their rears. They wore very high heeled shoes and were very exciting to watch and also very sexy. Goggles was fascinated by the leading lady and he decided that he would try to meet her after the show.

He kept to his decision and went backstage. He met her and paid her compliments for her performance. She was a singer as well as a dancer. He told her he was in the theatre business also and that pleased her. She smiled and said that she might meet him again but Goggles said that he would like to invite her to dinner with him in a posh hotel. She accepted the offer and he was tickled stiff that he had been successful in his strategy.

Later in the week, the dinner took place and it was just the first of countless meetings between the pair. The truth is that the romance continued, at a pace, for nine years before they married. He was about three years younger than she was.

During the nine years they travelled the world, in between work schedules and lived the high life, staying in exotic places and lavish hotels and eating and drinking the best. They earned good money and could afford such luxury.

Things took a turn for the worse back home in Pisheen West. Crappy's health broke down and he became very depressed. He was on a great deal of medication and could not sleep at night. He had nightmares and was often sleep-walking.

He was doing a line with a lady known as The Rocker and she broke it off and skipped to the Isle of Mann. That depressed him even more. His GP told him that his case was one of manic depression and that it was serious. He was drinking a great deal of alcohol and smoking like fury.

One morning in November there was no trace to be found of Crappy. The neighbours were concerned as they had not seen him for about a week. He would normally be visible in the fields or on the road. The Guards were called out and the locals joined them to search for Crappy. Sadly, they found him down in the local river, fully clothed. He had taken a no-return flight to the world beyond and would not be back.

On hearing the sad news, Goggles convinced his wife, Poppy that he would have to return home to Pisheen West and take over the place as otherwise the family continuity with it, would be lost. He did not want just to put it up for sale. This was a big decision to make. Poppy agreed, so they gave up their work in the theatre and club and came back to Pisheen.

Goggles hired a local man called The Curlew to do the work on the farm as he himself had much learning to do where farming was concerned. Poppy's parents had a big cheese-making business in England and she decided, now that they had a farm, to purchase some goats for their milk and she developed a business producing Goats' cheese. She had forty five excellent goats, and they did well as she had the family background in this kind of operation. It became a great success for them and the profit augmented the gains from the farms.

It is amazing what people can do when they have a bit of experience in any area of life. On the other hand, it is often foolish starting out on a road that is not familiar because the lack of knowledge can lead to failure and good money may have been invested in the venture also. There is no substitute for experience.

They had no family when they returned to Pisheen but now they have triplets to keep them busy. We can only hope, at this stage, that they will live happily, from now on, with the kids, the goats and the friendly characters of this scenic rural place – Pisheen West.

It is always very difficult in families when a member takes his or her own life. Sometimes, with the best care and attention, this can happen as there may not be any warning sign at all. If a serious health condition exists, other family members need to be extra vigilant. A bit of really good advice and communication can be helpful in preventing the worst. Sadly, lives were lost, in the past and it is quite common today also, even among the young.

The Attorney of Grumpymore

A man you should meet is The Attorney. He is a big man, outsize, well fed and not bad looking at all. You will meet him if you ever visit the townland of Grumpymore any day of the week. He has a reputation for being out on the roads all the time. He is very fond of walking and it brings him into contact with many people, especially those who are out in the fresh air with their dogs, great and small.

He is no way curious or nosey. He just likes good conversation. It gives him a chance to show off his learning. He likes to hear himself talking and he does not like to be interrupted. The locals know him and let him rave on.

The Attorney's house is situated on the brink of a small lake and one of his hobbies is fishing. He sometimes fishes from the banks but he also has a nice small boat and he uses it, in the better weather. He has lots of fishing rods and all kinds of bait. He is lucky in that the lake is well stocked with a variety of fish and he likes nothing better than taking the fish home and cooking them himself. He lives alone and never married, though he was on good terms with a lady from the village of Mossybeg, a redhead, but it never came to anything. She had a bad name around those parts for stealing things. He is better off without her. She could also drink like a fish.

You may be curious to know why he is known as The Attorney. When he speaks, his language is very legalistic and he maintains that he has a great knowledge of the Law. He uses terms such as: *the aforesaid, whereas, Subsection*

9, herein, thereafter, appropriate to and so on. People say that he is a pain in the head. He has a very solemn look, long-bearded, tanned all over with high black hat and dark sunnies.

It is said that he studied Law at one time in England but he never talks about that to the local people.

He has one sister and she lives with him but they do not speak. There is some barrier between them. Jack Sprat who is the local Gombeen-man explains that it is a question of finance distribution. The Attorney has plenty of dosh but he does not share it with his sister, Priscilla.

As a result, she has often to go without and feels very upset that her brother is so mean. She is threatening to leave the house and search for some tall, dark and handsome guy who will splash out on her, in a big way. This could be wishful thinking as she is no beauty, has a wrinkled face, bandy legs and a big spare tyre. She may be better remaining put and coaxing "The Attorney" to be a bit freer with the cash flow.

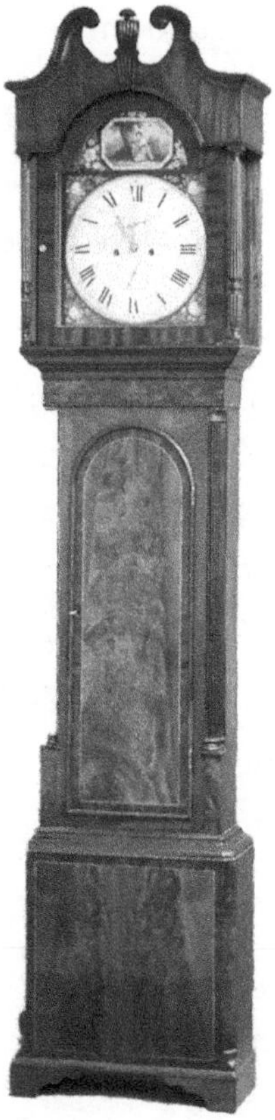

For a long time now The Attorney has been scouting the countryside, the cities and towns in search of clocks of all sorts, designs and sizes. He is addicted to them and his addiction is chronic. As of now, he has built up a massive collection of every conceivable type, size and design and he has them all preserved in what he calls his Time Zone which is a kind of museum. It is in an extension to his residence.

It is fascinating to go in there for a short spell to experience the dings, dongs, chimes, alarms, ticks and tocks of the various time pieces. Some are electrically powered but many have to be wound up manually. Some also have batteries. The Grandfather clocks dominate the place but there are many cuckoo clocks there too.

When the clatter builds up, you would think that you

are in a lunatic asylum, a serious threat to one's hearing. The collection is truly international, with specimens from all the continents. Beside each and every one of them is a short account of its design, together with its date and place of manufacture. The time conscious Attorney is proud of his assemblage and enjoys his addiction.

One night recently he was in the local community hall at a meeting of residents. After the Meeting an argument broke out between the Attorney and another man Pumpkin-head, over a court case that was in the news. The Attorney gave his decision as to what the result would be when the case would come to an end. Pumpkin-head disagreed and it eventually came to blows.

A fierce fight ensued. There was skin and hair flying, blood running down cheeks and great perspiration. Chairs were upturned, delph was smashed, glasses were hopping off the floor. The language was loud and dramatic.

Gobstopper, the local comedian was there and he was disgusted with the pair and he said that if they did not stop, he would take out his revolver and blow their heads off. That quietened them and they stopped and sat down, exhausted.

If there was ever an event that matched the name of the village, Grumpymore, this was it. Pumpkin-head was surely grumpy that night but The Attorney was even grumpier. Before they left for home Gobstopper got the pair to shake hands and to forget about the fracas. Now he had some coaxing to do.

When The Attorney got home to Priscilla he looked like something returning from World War III. She stared at him, said nothing and went off to bed. I would say that she was delighted he got a battering, but she kept it to herself. It was very likely a wise move.

When he got up in the morning and entered the kitchen for his breakfast, he had a face on him like Dracula and Priscilla burst out laughing and could not stop. She fell over against the sink and nearly broke bones. She was still laughing and had to work hard to get the smiles off her face.

His Lordship was watching her but he did not make any move to attack her. He sat down and drank his orange juice. Then he explained to her what had transpired the night before. He was convinced that if the argument went to court, the judge would agree with his stand. He kept consoling himself that he was right and Pumpkin-head was away off the mark.

He has now decided to give a series of Lectures on Clocks and Watches and all kinds of Timekeepers. Early booking is advisable, if you can afford the Admission.

The Wobbler and Dottie of Gluggernamuck

You may well have heard of a place called Gluggernamuck. It must be one of the last places God made. If you are ever looking for a road sign for it, you will not find it, because there are only a few miserable residences in it. You could easily fly by it and never notice it at all. The village name is less than impressive and would not excite one about its inhabitants.

In that quaint place lives a rare individual known widely as The Wobbler McGinty.

If you ever saw him out walking, you would have that one solved. To put it in a nutshell, when he walks he sways from left to right in a kind of zig-zag fashion, resembling a small boat tossed about in a stormy ocean. He is very extravagant on fuel, so to speak and uses up a great deal of energy. He is probably one of those who likes to bring the two sides of the road with him, if that is possible.

The Wobbler's past wasn't easy. His Dad was a stuntman and one day when he was a teenager, his Dad who was stunting in America, fell from a sixty storey building in Manhattan, New York and departed this world in dramatic fashion. When his mother heard of the disaster she drank the local pub dry and then committed suicide, the thinking being that it was better join him than to be hanging around in Gluggernamuck solo.

The Wobbler's sister lives with him and she is no treasure, to put it in fairly respectable language. The few neighbours call her Dottie and as Whiskers, the local barber quipped – *Her name fits her perfectly, down to the ground for she is the maddest yoke God ever assembled on two legs.* The Mug Finnegan agrees with him and adds that she is a proper lunatic when she fuels up with strong Spirits, Guinness and Red Bull. She is an idle good-for-nothing. She does no housework and just sits on top of the dust and dirt. She is a great admirer of things but it stops there.

Wobbler has a great collection of cookery books and recipes that he got from a daft sister of his in California whose married name was Alexandrina Scotsdale - Scratch. His aim in cooking is to keep it simple and tasty without embellishments. If you are thinking of coming along to this Diner, you are advised to bring with you medications for tummy upset, indigestion and diarrhoea.

If you ask Dottie for a rundown of her favourite food she will give it to you concisely, like a prescription – Black pudding three times a day – you could say every four hours. She loves buttermilk because it turns her on, but avoid her at those times.

Some fool told Dottie one day that she had a great voice. She might have but it is not at all for singing. It is far more suitable for tearing strips off someone, when she is high. She can be as contrary as forty cats and her temper can reach boiling point in a split second, as quickly as you could say *Jack Robinson.*

One stormy day in the month of November, cattle from the neighbour's land broke into Wobbler's piece of tillage. They somehow managed to cross the narrow river which was the dividing line between the two adjoining farms. When Wobbler saw the destruction he lost his head and his ranting would crack the rocks. His face got as red as a turkey cock and his blood pressure took an upward surge. His tongue almost set fire to the undergrowth with anger.

Next thing, Dottie came on the scene. Her entry into the fury was like the Queen of Sheeba, but far less polite. She was agitated to be sure. She at once called for an interview with her offending neighbour, that is Cissie Ramsbottom. The locals call her by another name – "Lightening", because she moves very fast and with great suddenness. She is little or no match at all for Dottie.

The encounter between them was brief. Dottie did not hold conversation with her at all. She just gave her a push, punched her in the face - hard - and Cissie landed on her rear end in the middle of the ice cold flowing stream. Silence there was not but a roar from the water! Dottie then exclaimed, like a monarch on the throne: *May the cold water experience teach you to take care of your wandering animals.* Poor Cissie, a harmful creation of God was reduced in stature by the ducking but she was clean now and would not have need of a bath or a shower for a long time after her immersion. She got a solitary lesson in Irish Water and it was completely free of charge.

I heard that when she got back home she dried herself and warmed up beside a good turf fire and drank some intoxicating liquid to further bring up the temperature. It must have been strong because she could be heard singing in the village of Sluggyville, a great distance away. Those who heard her thought that she was singing something from "Rigeletto" but Fiddler the Freckles, a good singer who dropped in, didn't join her for a duet because her voice carries. It surely does.

At this point, a bit of advice to would be visitors to Gluggernamuck might be a good thing. If you have any respect for yourself, do not visit this awful place or converse with any of its terrible inhabitants. Muldoon, the Sage, says: *When in the vicinity of this village, take a wide berth and sail out into quieter waters. You will be a winner then.* I think I will follow his advice.

It is amazing when one thinks of the way neighbours behave towards one another at times. Despite the fact that they live, side by side, for many years, when a small incident occurs, hell breaks loose between them. Very often it is just that cattle break into a garden or it may be a dispute over a right-of-way. It is hard to believe that such small happenings can lead to neighbours not talking to each other for years. They are foolish because, in due course, they die and leave it all after them. In those cases, love your neighbour has been deleted.

Disaster and the Rose of Gombeen

Today, I am going to tell you something of two very unlike characters. They are the married couple, Disaster and Pansie. It is difficult to know how they tagged on to each other as they are poles apart, in every respect.

They live in a two-storey house down in the village of Gombeen, a name that could suggest some connection with the aforementioned pair. It is good that the house has two storeys, because when things are a bit fiery, there is a bit of space for isolation.

The male portion of this twosome is Disaster. Now you may ask, why this name? They say that the local people christened this individual in such a way because there were many disasters in his life, and in addition, he never has a good news story, if you meet him. It is always a tale of woe, one kind of misfortune or another.

He is just dynamic when he talks about the weather.

The picture in Winter is always one of utter desolation as he predicts the Last judgment. You can see, in your mind's eye, fire and brimstone , thunder and lightening and even an earthquake about to happen.

In Summer, he turns on a different recording. The long dry spell is a sign of great disaster, heat building up, the earth cracking open, drought and possible famine later, crops wilting, water shortage, huge fires to take hold of the woods and the boglands, fire brigades under extreme pressure and people likely to die from the heat and exhaustion not to mention drownings as people try to cool themselves down.

This is only a taste of his presentation and as Teaser Tim put it: *That man is a pain in the intestines. He would crack your head with his vocabulary. He is bad enough on a Summer's day but he is a hell of a lot worse in the middle of Winter. He should be locked up.*

Pansie is a different type altogether. She is quite fancy and spends ages rubbing powder into her face and bathing it with milk. She has five big mirrors and when she does not like what she sees in one, she switches on to another which may give her a more acceptable result. As Julia Kikker remarked recently: *It makes no difference what make-up she uses or what mirror she uses, there is nothing of any account there with which to start. She is as ugly as the rear end of an elephant.*

Pansie rides a motorbike and when she takes to the highways she moves. When the children coming home from school hear her coming, they jump over the ditches for safety. She has a hooter on the flying machine and she knocks the daylights out of it, to let the neighbours know that she is airborne. She says herself that she would be lost without her bike. Molly the Crock said: *That would be mighty. Who would want to find her? I have a good mind to steal her ould bike myself.*

I want to fill you in on something from Disaster's life. He has had his own share of bad happenings, down the years. He lost all his cattle one year when they were hit by lightening. He got a heart attack after that and was laid up for a year and a half.

He had just one son and he worked in England, on the buildings. One day, He fell down from scaffolding, and he about ten storeys up and was killed. It took him years to recover from that tragic event.

He got insurance money later, but it did him no good because he hit the bottle and that nearly finished him off altogether. Worse still, Pansie got into the bad habit also and it did her health no good. She put on weight and was bulging all over.

The local quack Whizzer diagnosed her condition but no one believed what he said about her. They took it that he must be only joking. What he said was: *Pansie has gearbox trouble and she needs to have it sorted out or it could kill her without any warning. That's it, in a nutshell.*

Disaster himself used to drive an old Ford car but it came to a sad end one night there was a heavy frost. On his way home from the local pub, it went into some kind of a war dance, spun around on the road and straight into the river Grimey, hitting a stone wall before doing so. He managed to get out of the vehicle because the river was not too deep, at that point. He was in a a state of shock for some weeks after that and he did not drive anymore. The car was a write-off and the locals say that Pansie then bought the motorbike as she did not want to be totally stranded.

There is a very daft lady in the village called Popoff and she sets herself up as a kind of adviser to anyone who might be silly enough to listen to her. One evening, some time ago, she happened to meet Pansie and the conversation was all about the advertised Rose of Gombeen competition. It was for over forties only. Popoff convinced Pansie that she should enter for it. She got such a conditioning that she could hardly refuse to do so.

Well, when the locals heard the news, their eyes opened very wide, there was a look of wonder on their faces and they said that it was necessary to get the opinion of the guy in the village called "The Crank" to pronounce on it.

Biddy Paudie Peats got the task of contacting The Crank. He was making soup when she called, oxtail with croutons. He is more often gruff, contrary and weasel-like.

When he got details of the Rose competition he broke into loud laughter and he couldn't stop. He nearly choked himself and fell over against the dresser.

When he calmed down he delivered his verdict: *I would recommend that she withdraw from this circus, for a number of reasons. She has not got the statistics required to have any chance of even being selected or short-listed. Let me spell this out a little. First of all, she is far too short. She has not got the legs required to make an impression. The ones she has are as crooked as the bend on the road outside. She does not seem to have any noticeable rear end and her hips are too spread out, like an expanding balloon. Up front, she is as flat as the Nevada Desert and as to her face, it's the Dracula type, frightening, with a bulge that resembles a rugby ball, well inflated.*

Biddy Paudie Peats got it from the horse's mouth and returned to her friends with the verdict. Now, the expert on women had spoken, so the locals decided to divert Pansie from the competition. They advised her that she could not turn up for it on her motorbike, wearing a long frock, unless she wished to go in her outsize bikini. She listened and then asked how she could travel.

A real prankster in the village offered to drive her, on the night, and so he did. As it happened, the night was very foggy and as the Hall where the competition was being held was a good distance away, the driver told Pansie before he set off with her, that it seemed to him that it would be a dirty night and they might not make it to the Hall.

She urged him to push on and take pot luck. After about fifteen minutes into the journey, the fog worsened and you could not see a thing, but the driver moved on again. Suddenly, there was a loud noise coming from under the car, at the back. On examination, there was a flat tyre and there was no spare wheel to rectify the problem.

The driver informed her that the case was hopeless and could not be rectified until morning. He delayed for a good while before he went to a nearby house and explained the situation. They had no car but said that they could ring Mutton, one of their lads and that he had cars and would have a spare wheel.

It seemed ages before it arrived and was fitted. This was all arranged so that Pansie would be late for the judging. By the time they got to the Hall they met the crowd going home. She was distraught and broke down crying but said that what happens is best. She was listening to the people returning from the event and heard them talking about the winner.

The driver asked one of the women who actually won. He was informed that the winner was John James Vincent's daughter, the one the locals call The Giraffe. She is six feet and four inches tall and not a pick on her. You could use her to knit an Aran sweater, a proper knitting needle.

Pansie was taken home and went on brandy for a fortnight to recover from the disappointment.

Disaster kept well clear of all the carry-on and warned herself that if she did not quit the brandy and sober up, he would commit suicide. That scared her and she gave up the drink.

Having lost out in the beauty stakes, she got into bee-keeping and marketed her honey in the local shops. One night someone stole her motorbike which was parked outside in a dark space. She never got it back.

Many believed that some local stole it, to put her off the road. There was one major suspect, namely, The Quilt Flynn, but he was never seen with the motorbike. The mystery remains unsolved.

I heard last evening that Disaster died a week ago - a second heart attack. Pansie is now left minus her mode of transport and Disaster, to paddle her own canoe.

She has taken herself off to a Health Farm now, to get some detox, to learn the art of healthy living and to have some bit of social life, meeting people and encouraging sales of her own products. She is convinced that there is real goodness in honey and she keeps rooting for the welfare of her bees all the while. Let us hope that she does not get seriously stung!

God bless the pair of them. I suppose it takes all sorts to people the planet.

The Little Professor – Thelma Snuff

There is a village in a valley called Woodlands and in it lives a little woman the locals call The Little Professor. Her real name is – Thelma Snuff.

The reason for this title is that she is very learned, well read and she has travelled the world and has seen interesting places. She does not believe in keeping the information to herself. She likes to share it with others in her village and in the wider area around.

In Winter she draws up a Programme which she calls *Informative Talks.* They deal with various places and topics and she invites everyone interested to come along to her cosy residence to hear what she has to say.

She is delighted when she sees the children and teenagers attending in big numbers. They feel that the information will help their education and examinations. Of course, the adults come in also and love her musings.

She deals with just one topic at a time and gives her Presentations on two nights per week, namely, on Mondays and on Thursdays. The time required is usually an hour and she takes questions from her audience afterwards.

She is a decent and generous woman and she always has a treat for the youngsters such as snacks and soft drinks. The adults get tea or coffee and homemade scones. The good news is that it is all free.

The night I dropped in, her chosen topic was *The Wild Atlantic Way.* I did not record it but the following is my recollection of the key points she mentioned:

As far as I can recall she began her trip with Kinsale and The Ring of Kerry: *Kinsale is my starting point this evening. It is a very attractive town on the south coast of Ireland, on the Bandon River with two 17th century fortresses overlooking it. It is a colourful harbour town with its boats, hotels and restaurants, popular with tourists.*

She mentioned Kenmare with its lovely well-kept town and bay, then Sneem, small but beautiful, and on to Waterville, Caherciveen and Killorglin, observing on route Dingle Bay and Valentia Island. She referred to the Blasket Islands, home of many literary figures such as Tomás Ó Criomhthin, Peig Sayers and Muiris Ó Súilleabháin.

She went on to say that the West Coast of Ireland is stunningly beautiful, long, varied and winding and it is undoubtedly wild. There, land and ocean meet and the sky above it is its canopy. To drive it, from Kerry to Donegal is both challenging and exciting. As one travels along, the scene changes all the time, maintaining interest and curiosity, without fail.

The scenery is impressive and the views are limitless. The roads present a challenge for the driver in question. They twist and loop around the land features and they tend to be narrow, so full concentration is required. There are many stopping points along the Way, for a break and some photographs and above all, to take in the fabulous views. Make sure that you select a fine, dry, sunny day. Otherwise, you will be wasting your time.

In Co. Limerick you can visit Foynes and its seaport and historic Limerick city by the famous Shannon. You can drop in to see Bunratty Castle and Folk Park.

In Co. Clare there is much choice of venues. Visit the town of Kilrush, Loop Head and Kilkee before going northwards to Doonbeg with its bay and river and the spectacular Cliffs of Moher, visited by thousands of tourists ever year. Travelling northwards, pop into Spanish Point, Miltown-Malbay and Lahinch. Allow yourself plenty of time to admire the vast expanse of the Burren. Tread on its limestone pavements and rocks and look beyond to catch a glimpse of the Aran Islands in the distance and the wide expanse of the Atlantic Ocean.

The Burren or boireann, in Gaelic, means a rocky place. When Cromwell was in Ireland he said that the Burren did not have enough soil in which to bury a man, enough water in which to drown a man or enough wood to hang a man.

That may be so, but this terrain is unique and often referred to as a Karst Landscape, predominantly limestone, having similarities with the Dinaric Alps in the former Yugoslavia, along the Adriatic Coast.

The Burren landscape is ancient and has many interesting Neolithic features, dolmens and caves and an underground drainage system. It is famous overseas for its variety of exotic plants and flowers and botanists visit it every year. Animals graze on parts of it.

Driving along the south shore of Galway Bay, you soon approach Galway City itself and famed Salthill. Visit University College, Galway,the Cathedral and harbour area. From there it is on to Connemara, a true wilderness of rocks, mountains, lakes and vistas. There, you can let your imagination wander back in time. Admire the heather-clad boglands and the features of Ireland's glacial past. Listen to the local people speaking the Irish language and observe their way of life today.

Next up is Co. Mayo with Clew Bay and all its islands, majestic Croagh Patrick where our patron saint fasted and prayed and touristic Westport town, always flower-bedecked and beautiful to visit. From Bertra Beach, look across the bay to see the Nephin Beg Mountain Range and Nephin Mór before heading for Newport, Mulranny and Achill Island with its cliffs, beaches and rural villages.

Travelling northwards, visit Bangor Erris, Belmullet and the Mullet

Peninsula. Do not miss the Céide Fields before arriving in Killala.

On to Ballina with its River Moy.

Continue on to Co. Sligo with its coastal beaches of Enniscrone, Strandhill and Rosses Point. Visit at least some of the places associated with the poet, William Butler Yeats and his poetry – Knocknarea Mountain, Lough Gill, the Lake Isle of Innisfree, Lissadell House, Drumcliffe Churchyard to see the grave of the famous poet with his epitaph: *Cast a cold eye on life, on death. Horseman, pass by.*

Last but not least comes Co. Donegal, another gem with its great coastline and beaches, majestic mountains such as Errigal, fabulous scenery and attractive towns and villages, not to mention warm friendly, welcoming people.

You have many options. You can visit Donegal town itself, Bundoran, high and wild, Ballyshannon, Killybegs, Glenties, Buncrana, Glencolumcille and many more.

Get a glimpse of the coastal islands of Arranmore and Tory, the former made famous in a song – The Rose of Arranmore.

It suits some people to begin the journey in Kinsale, Co. Cork and end up in Co. Donegal. Others may decide to travel from there south to Kinsale.

There are also those who may travel only sections of the entire route. There are five Sections in total – Cork to Kerry; Kerry to Clare; Clare to Mayo; Mayo to Donegal and Donegal itself.

The entire route is 2,500 kms or 1,553 miles long. For this reason, allow plenty of time to take it all in. One could spend an entire month on this route but it is possible to do it all, with stops, in a week to ten days.

Along the route there are 157 discovery points, 1000 attractions and 2,500 activities. It connects three of Ireland's four provinces, namely, Munster, Connaught and Ulster.

I hope I have managed to capture the more important things that the Little

Professor mentioned in her Presentation. There can be no doubt but that the *Wild Atlantic Way drive* is a classic and probably the best in the world. We should be proud to have it in Ireland for it is truly unique.

Visit it, if you can and experience the passage of time, its sights, sounds and colours and its lovely fresh Atlantic air. When you have experienced it, you should have no difficulty in believing in God, for it is a wonderful creation that goes beyond the human.

A word of warning for those who may not be experienced drivers. It is not a route for learners or novices, so please take note of that. The reason for saying this is that most of the route is quite narrow, winding and as a result, challenging to drive it safely. Take breaks and equip yourself with a good map.

I should tell you before I finish that I got a great cup of coffee and a hot scone from the fine little lady that is affectionately known as The Little Professor.

The Critical Humanity Lecture

By Professor Jake "Big Ears" McGoo, D.Litt.
University of Freckley.

Good evening everyone! Welcome to my Lecture reflecting on the human race today. I hope to shed some light on this fascinating topic and during my exposition, you are free to respond, heckle or just remain silent. You may drink water or other liquids, eat sweets and crisps, but do make an effort to listen to what I have to say.

To begin with, let me say that there are two major categories of humans in the world, namely, the good and the bad. The latter group is much bigger than the former, so I will deal with it firstly. The bad are often bad because they have less of everything than the good and for this reason, they spend a good deal of their time trying to take their possessions from them, so that they themselves will have a better life.

Because the methods used by them are illegal they run into great difficulties and may end up in prison or may even get killed. They are, however, prepared to take a chance as they usually have nothing else to do. They are very active and never seem to give up.

The proof of this is the fact that the news bulletins are saturated with criminality every single day. The people who act as they do, must be unhappy in themselves, especially when they are arrested, brought to court, thrown into jails and so on. Even after all of that, they still continue to break the law.

Those people get into their bad ways due to a faulty upbringing where parents had no control over their children and the family was very likely disadvantaged, in some way, deprived of resources. employment and even education.

In recent times, we have no difficulty in seeing badness in our world, many dastardly acts of violence, carried out by awful leaders against their own people and others, involving shootings, hangings, killings, ethnic cleansing, in one way or another. Ruthless, despotic tyrants have existed, for long in many countries, dictators who act like demons, with no regard for human life at all. This is particularly true of countries in Africa, South America and Asia.

The good, on the other hand, have come a different road. They are people who probably got a good start in life, had plenty of everything, property, money, schooling, employment and much more. They would not have experienced want or the many problems of the other category. Many of the good appreciate their status and often share their wealth with the poor, through the various charitable organisations or through initiatives of their own, and so contribute much to the living conditions of the deprived. If more help were given, there would be less criminality in the world.

If you travel around the world you will see, in all countries of repute, any amount of monuments and statues of people who made a great contribution, in their day, to the life of their countries. Their goodness and abilities shone out and have lived on, after them. Some of them may have been great leaders, writers, musicians, architects, painters, sculptors, poets, saints. They leave us in no doubt but that there has been good in our world and they have left it a better place than it was, prior to their contribution.

There is a great imbalance in the world between rich and poor nations and the rich ones could do much better than at present to alleviate poverty in the poorer nations. Big sums of money are spent on many useless projects that should be given to the poorer nations to help them get on their feet. There is a certain amount of selfishness, an ambition for prestige, dominance and power. There should be more generosity and common sense from leaders and Governments.

One would expect that Religion should be a force for good in the world, but if one looks at the history of the world there has been a clash between different religious groups, one wanting to dominate and undermine the other or to draw new members for itself. There should not be any such thing as competition between religions. There should be freedom for all and respect for all. Generally, there is some good in all religions, so tolerance is required.

As well as the good and the bad in the world there is another in-between group which is neither bad nor good. They can be indifferent to many things and have a mentality of their own. They think that Society owes them a living and that they should get everything for free from the State while they contribute little or nothing to it, in terms of taxes or even employment. Whenever there is a major issue in the news, they will always be seen taking part in parades and protest marches on the streets of cities. They will have big placards highlighting their grievances and sometimes cause trouble when clashes take place with the police. If other people behaved like them, what would countries come to?

They need to learn a lesson or two. Society does not owe them a living and they should reflect upon that truth. Those people are not to be equated with Society's poor who deserve our sympathy and support. Christianity demands this of all of us, for blessed are the poor in spirit.

One of the very nasty aspects of the modern world is the lack of respect for human life, both outside and inside the womb. Life seems to have no value and therefore it can be disposed of, at will. Humans act as if they were God and take the law into their own hands. They are despots too and they must be reprimanded and controlled. Unfortunately, there is a percentage of the population in countries who want everything regulated to suit their own particular view, be they right or wrong. We see this all the time, where very controversial issues are being debated or decided upon, like for example, the question of Abortion.

In that case, they want a free-for-all situation. That must never be allowed to happen because no one has a right to take anyone's life, whether it be walking the street or a child in the womb. God alone has that right and people who may be campaigning for a free-for-all situation in regard to this matter, should quit the nonsense and ask themselves why they want this. It is pure selfishness and it is actually murder of a human being. If that happened to themselves, they would never have seen the light of day. They should think about that.

Do people who advocate Abortion ever ask themselves why they are always pushing for it. There is a much better approach to this and it is absolutely positive. Peoples' own behaviour must be changed. By that I mean, if certain people do not want to give birth to a child, then they should not get pregnant, should not be sexually involved with another. That calls for a personal responsibility, thoughtfulness and discipline.

The easy way out, namely, abortion, is the wrong way out. If they find themselves pregnant, they must take the consequences and ensure that the child or children, in some cases, are born, in the normal and natural way.

The pro-abortion grouping lacks maturity and education in basic moral principles and they do not want to listen to reason at all. All Life is sacred and God alone is its Author.

I often wonder does anyone ever learn anything from history. We have had many awful wars down the centuries, with terrific loss of life and the sad thing is that wars are still occurring and little devils of dictators are stlll posing threats to peace in the world. They need to be removed, without any delay as otherwise, they may cause a disaster of world proportions.

As you can gather from what I have said, the human race is a very mixed bag and for that reason, there is need for great patience, tolerance and common sense, even a sense of humour in dealing with situations.

There is one thing very lacking in the modern world and that is a sense of humour. It is necessary, in many situations as it can diffuse tension, keep people relaxed and it can help to ensure that friendships can develop. Even the Pope has commented on the lack of humour today. People are going around with very gloomy faces, all tensed up and afraid to soften down, to relax a bit and smile. Humour is a therapy and it costs nothing. It is up to people themselves to cultivate it. When it is combined with common sense, you have the perfect ingredient for successful living. There you have a combination which will and does contribute, in no small way, to a person's wellbeing.

Thank you for your attention to my Lecture. I hope you enjoyed my remarks. Of course, you do not have to agree with anything I have said. The good news now is, as I have been told by the University authorities, that you may avail of some fish and chips and a soft drink in the Headers' Restaurant in Block 999. Enjoy!

Mamma's Letter to her Daughter "Midge" in Sydney

Cloonscatty North,
Bowelstown.

Wednesday.

My dearest Midge,

I am writing to update you on happenings here since you left for Sydney, down under. You must be up-side-down, down there, but you will get used to it, after a while.

I suppose you are over the jet-lag by now and your head will be clearer. You need a clear head in a strange country, not that I am ever clear-headed myself, with all the health problems I have. I will come to them later, but firstly, I will update you on the latest news here. When abroad, it is nice to know what is going on back home, not that this place is a roaring metropolis.

The Bully Brennan was killed yesterday when his tractor turned over on a steep slope. It rolled down the hill and he fell off the tractor, hitting his head off a rock. The rock is undamaged but the tractor is a write off. He will be greatly missed by Minty, the wife.

Elsie Mac's two sisters are home from Philadelphia. You know them, the daft ones who were always done up to kill, but nothing on top , I mean no brain of any kind. They are still the same, no improvement. They smoke like bad chimneys in the Wintertime. They will never get men because they are too fancy and could never rough it in this or in any other country.

Doomsday is building an Aviary, a place where he will have all kinds of exotic birds, of the feathery type. He is rotten with money. He will drive us out of our minds with the squeaking and squaking, if we are not there already.

The pair down the road, Skimmed Milk himself and Parsley herself had an unmerciful fight recently. There was skin and hair flying and you could light the fire with the heat of the language. He ended up with multiple scrapes on his face and neck, so he is not for viewing at the moment. She has two black eyes which gives her a tough look but they are not pretty. They never hit it off at any time and now and again, there are eruptions that get out of hand. They are both very headstrong individuals. They always remind me of active volcanoes.

A gang of gurriers raided Dancer Mulligan's farm recently and stole his machinery and expensive tools. He was so shocked that he had to be brought to the hospital where he spent a week recovering . The wife, Glimmer went on a dose of tranquilisers and was seeing things in her sleep. She thought she was a monster going around devouring anything that came in her way. Of course, you know as I know, that she was never the full shilling anyway, a bit of a cracked pot, so to speak.

All Molly Jack's hens are laying big eggs, all free range and she is stuffing herself with them now for some time, boiled, fried, poached and scrambled. No danger that she would share them with the neighbours. She is as mean as my boot. Well, we can all manage without her, thank God.

You know the Scientist who lived over in the Scollops' area . He is known as "Punch Face". Well, he was carrying out an experiment that he had been working on in his laboratory. Then he went outside to test a small rocket that he hoped to launch from his elaborate set-up in his garden. He got into the rocket and then his assistant Cringer pressed all the required buttons to start the launch. The rocket took off but after a short ascent it burst into flames and fell back down to earth with his nibs inside. By the grace of God Cringer managed to release him from the gadget and he avoided injury.

A Yank visited our village recently and came to the conclusion that everyone around here barring myself and your father is a luper and not fit for purpose. Well, I can tell you that he is no rock of sense himself, slugging glasses of whiskey and eating his big cigars. He had me almost smothered in smoke, the ugly bragger. You would know to whom he is related, Crazy Kitty, the lady with the hump and the big red nose, down there in Madramore.

To come now to myself. As you know my health is not good. I have a problem sleeping at night. I only get about two hours and after that I have to get up and make tea. Sleeping pills kill me altogether, so I do not take them anymore. I sit up for ages reading the local newspapers, looking out for all the juicy bits and the scandals. You know my form Midge.

My ankles are swollen so I have difficulty walking around. I bathe them in hot water, now and again. I am overweight or obese as they say now. I have a craving for chocolate and whiskey but the latter makes me feel good and brave. I am also getting uglier by the day. The wrinkles are showing. Ginger Nut said that I must be getting ready for the role of Dracula in the forthcoming production down in the Hall. In fairness, I have given up things such as fat salty bacon, black and white pudding, cakes and soft drinks. I am greatly out of breath and I get the "Runs" a few times a day. "Clocker" has advised a complete refurbishment of my system, and he is right.

Turning to yourself, Midge I hope you like Sydney. It is unlike our village but you should go to see the Opera House , not that you were ever into Opera or even music, for that matter. Clocker was in Australia once and he went to see Aires Rock. He was trying to climb up to the top of it but slipped, fell down and broke his leg, in two places. If you go there, no climbing I say. You might also pop up to see the Great Barrier Reef but do not put a leg in the water as it is full of tropical weirdos.

The underwear you had going down there was not very fancy, so you might look around the shops there for more suitable stuff. Keep your skirts down a bit as you wear them too short. Less ventilation is better, especially in cold weather. An overdose of exposure to the scenery might be dangerous. You know me and my ideas. Furthermore, you could end up with a bad flu or even pneumonia.

Be careful with the company you keep as there are many vultures out there. Do not budge an inch, in any tight corner and when out keep your money in your bra. Take no chances and do not be out late at night, on your own. I am ruling out completely any liaison with fellows, no matter how handsome. Sometimes, the miserable -looking ones are the worst. Bid them off, if they approach. Tell them your mother is just around the corner and she is dangerous as she has a gun and some knives. Now, you cannot say that you have not been warned.

One other thing! I am banning all alcoholic drink but it is fine to drink the usual, tea, coffee, hot chocolate, water and soft drinks. By the way, I am also banning smoking. You were never into the fags but you might be thinking of starting now. I say NO to that. You know where I stand, Midge. Good girl you are! Take Mamma's advice and you will climb to great heights down there. You know that I came up the hard way.

Put pen to paper as soon as you are organised and let me know all the latest news from down under. I must hurry now and feed the turkeys as we are fattening them up for sale at or around the Christmas. The cat and dog here are also looking up at me for some food and the calves in the paddock are lowing for a bit of hay, not to mention the pigs in the sty scraping the door for a bit of nourishment as well. The cock is crowing in the yard. He is the spokesman for the hens and they are all starving out there. Jesus, Mary and Joseph help me. It is well for you to be away from this mayhem.

I will close off now and I will be on the lookout for your reply before long. O yes, I nearly forgot, if you have any spare dollars, slip them into the envelope, before you seal it.

With warm and best wishes.

Your concerned Mamma,

Millie.

Down on the Farm with Jazzi May Dan

If you ever come anyway near the sprawling village of Sloshmore Upper, you should give Jazzie May Dan a shout. She would love the fact that you called to see her in action.

It is not easy to describe her as she is into every type of job on the farm, big and small. As Luke the Gander said about her – *She is a man of a woman.* Annie May McHugh of the famous Ploughing Championships would love her, for she can put a gloss on the brown sods that she turns over in what she calls the Riverside field. She is no mean plougher.

When her cows are calving, she is there with them, pulling the calves and she does all the milking too, with the aid of milking machines. She has a total of thirty five cows and they need hay, bales and silage to sustain them, in Winter and she always has plenty of calves to care for, cleans their barns or sheds and gives them hay and meals, from day to day.

She makes the silage herself and also does the baling. She never grumbles and seems to be happy doing what she does. She loves to sing as she goes about her business and as I heard her at it, I can say that she has a good voice.

Jazzie May is a great sheep-shearer and she never leaves a blemish on the sheep's skin. She wraps up the fleeces with precision and style. She also transports the wool to a buyer she knows down in Drakeland. She is a good wheeler and dealer when it comes to selling her products.

She brings her cattle to the local Mart in her trailer and she drives her big tractor with skill. She has four colourful flags hanging out of it for effect and she also sports some fancy lights on the front and rear of the vehicle. Dopey Billberry has christened her "Queen of the Mart". She is often the only female present among an ocean of men, but that does not ruffle her one bit.

Her only helper is her dog, Bruno who is of great assistance when she wants to round up the cattle or sheep. When the Vet calls to tag the cattle, he is very active as he is when she grooms him and even takes him for a walk, on a regular basis.

Jazzie is adept when it comes to machinery. She can handle all the various machines she has, such as the combine-harvester, hay-tedder, muck-spreader, rotavator, mowers, ploughs, fork lifts, slurry tank, sprayer, small diggers and even her JCB.

Jazzie has a Mercedes and driving it is an easy task after the big machines. She does not go on holidays but she strolls down to Laughing Larry's Pub, every night where she enjoys several pints of Guinness and converses with the locals. She has plenty of money earned on her farm and she inherited much wealth also from an uncle who was nicknamed *Sideways* because of the way he walked, never in a straight line, which is the shortest distance between two points, as we know. He made his money out in the Persian Gulf, in the oil business.

Jazzie has no interest in men. She says they are only a distraction and they always want to be in control of everything. She prefers to be independent and to be her own boss. Life, she says is much easier that way. That is fine for her but if every other woman thought like that, the population of countries would be in crisis.

As time goes on she may well change her mind as she has opportunities to meet fellows who would be willing to have such a good worker and such a successful woman, on the land. She is a member of the local rugby club and plays rugby on a regular basis. She is very fit and that contributes to her good health and stamina. Neighbours have been advising her that she should make life easier for herself by employing a bit of help on the farm but she does not seem to go along with the suggestion. As she gets older, she may agree with it.

Some time ago she qualified as a mechanic and this is a plus for her as she is able to service all her machinery herself. She has a pit in one of her sheds and she can drive the tractor and other machines in over it and then go down and change oils and do repairs, as the case may be.

She even obliges some of the neighbours by doing servicing for them also. She has a good name among them for her decency and generosity. Her best friend in the village is Eyelashes Mulligan and she is great craic, always telling yarns which should be censored but she gets away with them.

The two of them go down to the Leisure Centre, twice a week and enjoy a swim, the sauna, jacuzzi and steam room. They are both good swimmers and have taken part in competitions and won prizes for their performances.

Another aspect of her farm is her beautiful flower garden which she has built up over a number of years. It is very large and she has many exotic plants and flowers in it. There are nice pathways through it and she has many small trees and shrubs forming a background for the flowers. It is quite a task keeping them watered when there are long dry spells. It is pleasant just to walk through this lovely space and the scent from the flowers is heavenly. Bees and butterflies hover around and the birds in the trees belt out their own symphony.

Last year Jazzie May and Eyelashes went on a trip to the Netherlands as she wanted to see how the Dutch grow their daffodils and other flowers. She brought home many good ideas and the pair also went to the Chelsea Flower Show because they had heard good reports of it. They have also been to Bloom in the Phoenix Park, a number of times.

My conclusion, after my research into Jazzie May Dan is that she is an excellent performer on her farm who keeps up-to-date and is a great example for other women who might be thinking of taking up farming. It is good to see today many young women doing Courses in agriculture with a view to becoming professional farm managers. That is a big change from the times past and it is a trend that should be encouraged.

Centenarian Matilda Talks to the School Children

Good afternoon children! "Good afternoon, Matilda"!

I promised you that I would talk to you about myself and the years I have lived through. As you know, I am just turned one hundred years of age, so I am ancient now and there is a big gap between where I am and where you are at.

I was born in a little thatched house in this village of Cloontruflish. I heard later that there were several feet of snow on that day. I was the last in a family of twenty three. No family today is like that. Nowadays, there are only two or three children in many families, sometimes only one.

Many women had very hard lives then. Not only were the families big, but life was tough in other respects also. It was a very simple kind of lifestyle. There was no grandeur, no luxuries, little money, nothing in the houses to make for lighter, easier work in the home.

There was not even electricity, just candles or paraffin lamps for light. That meant that a woman in her kitchen had to make do with pots, pans and ovens placed over a turf fire to do some cooking. Bread was made by placing a cake of oaten meal on a griddle, with red hot coals under it to bake it. Sometimes, the cake was put into an oven with coals from the fire placed on top of the lid and also underneath.

On farms, much of the food people ate came from the land. It was plain but the quality was good. There were plenty of vegetables, potatoes, home cured bacon, because many homes killed pigs, free range eggs, poultry such as, geese, turkeys and ducks. There was a good supply of milk and butter was made at home, in a churn.

People who did not live on farms, lacked these foodstuffs and depending on supplies from the shops was not great because they often lacked grocery items, for one reason or another.

Young people like you today do not understand how backward Ireland was a hundred years ago. Technology did not exist so there were no radios of any account, no television, no I-Pads, I–Phones, smart phones, decent cameras or any state-of-the-art gadgets. You do not realise how well-off you are, with all this luxury that you take for granted, but there may be a down-side to some of this also.

When people had spare time such as in the Winter with the long nights, they sat by the fire and had great conversations. They told stories and knew everyone in the locality, who married who and who the people were before them. The Seanchaí or storyteller was the star and he really entertained.

Irish music was played in people's homes and young and old danced to the music. The hooleys were usually in the kitchens. Dancing also took place at the crossroads because it was easy for people to gather where the roads crossed each other.

The down-side of today's technology may leave young people without any ability to converse with others as their heads are stuck in the phones all the time, texting and using social media. They will not be able to write or spell words properly as texting has become a disease, almost and English as a subject in school will undoubtedly suffer. Results in State examinations are already showing up this problem.

The standard of education in the primary schools was good, in the past, as all the basic things were well taught. Reading, spelling, writing and mathematics were emphasised. The children's hand-writing was beautiful. History, geography and catechism were also drummed into the pupils, as was, Irish and English.

There was no place for any fancy stuff or nonsensical entertainment- type diversions like you have today. Schooling was a serious business then, not something that was just meant to be fun. It was good that things were like that because primary schooling was all many young people got then. They often emigrated to England or America after that.

Going along the road, people had plenty of time to stop and talk, when they met neighbours or others. There was no clock-watching, no pressure. Time did not seem to enter into people's lives.

Today, everyone seems to be stressed out all the time, under pressure, always watching the clock, running here and there, driving here and there, speeding from Billy to Jack and back again, exhausted, on tranquilisers, medications and hospitals bulging at the seams with sick people and massive waiting lists.

One is inclined to think that, despite all the good food and pampering today, we must have a very poor standard of health in Ireland. There were no waiting lists in Ireland a hundred years ago because there were no elaborate hospitals in the country then, but people lived more normal, healthy and relaxed lives.

They were not bombarded with high-powered advertising as is the case today. There were less distractions and less mobility as cars were few and far between. The donkey and cart were far more common.

One result of this was that men could not travel long distances to meet girls to marry so they often married girls who were their neighbours or living in nearby villages. Because of emigration, the girls were often not around as they had left for employment in other countries. That left many men on their own and they had to live as bachelors for the rest of their lives.

Today, the Rat Race is on for more grandeur, more wealth, more status.

The older generators were not into those things and they had a great deal of common sense and humanity about them. Today, money has become God and God is pushed down the list, as a result.

Country people were great for helping one another. You may have heard of a Meitheal. That was where neighbours gathered together to help a family with work on the farm when they might not be in a position to do the work themselves. This was an example of loving your neighbour.

In times past, the Catholic Church was very powerful in Ireland and it exercised great discipline. Things then were black or white and everyone went to Mass and the Sacraments, attended Sodalities, kept the Commandments and scandal was frowned upon. People involved were treated as outcasts which was very severe. Old Irish society could be cruel because it was born out of hard warlike times.

First Communion was treated with great dignity and simplicity. There was no big show-off with fancy outfits, limousines or lavish parties afterwards. Pocket money was given to the children but it was always modest.

When Confirmation time arrived things were the same, no parade of stylish outfits, no school uniforms, no big meals or celebrations afterwards. Common sense prevailed so no one had to worry about keeping up with the Jones's.

When Christmas came around, Santa Claus came but all kids got were small items stuffed into a stocking which was left hanging from the mantelpiece over the fireplace. The stocking might contain such things as an apple, oranges, sweets, chocolate, toy soldiers, a comic, water gun and so on. There were no large exotic toys, no electrical, mechanical or technological items like today. Despite this, kids then were happy enough because they were not accustomed to luxuries. They often were pleased to play with a football or even a cardboard box.

Parents, in days gone by were very strict with the youngsters and demanded that they did what they were told. They had great control, unlike many cases today, where youngsters call the shots and later end up badly because they did not do what they were told.

The strict discipline of the past has given way now to a softly, softly, approach which has led to a break-down in discipline, in many situations which, sadly, ends up in some kind of criminality. All you have to do is listen to the news on television or radio and you will see that most of it is about shootings, stabbings, robberies, break-ins and court cases.

One is inclined to ask – Whatever happened to our island of saints and scholars? There is something very wrong with a Society that is producing so much of this kind of activity. The root causes should be identified and everything should be done to eliminate such behaviour. Much of it arises from bad family situations, deprivation, unemployment, poor housing, lack of education and an absence of discipline.

There is also another side to all of this. The desire to acquire wealth, by illegal means, leads to drug and other types of trafficking, causing competition between factions or groups and then the trouble starts and life is not sacred any more.

No right Society should allow this kind of behaviour to operate in our cities and towns or anywhere. Lack of resources is given as the reason for this continuing but, of course, this is not acceptable and people should not tolerate the ongoing misfortune which brings such a bad name on our country. If our forebears came back today, they would not be pleased and if our 1916 leaders came back, they would say that this is not the Ireland they died for, with great generosity.

Many bad traits developed in people in this country during the so-called Tiger Years such as arrogance, greed, bad tempers, lack of faith, poor or no Church attendance, disregard for basic principles and extravagant opulence and grandeur. Out with them!

Despite all the distractions and pressures on young people today, many are very hard workers and want to progress in life. They are very talented also, very open to ideas and they care for their parents, friends and neighbours.

I know that you here in Cloontruflish want to do your best. I have just been giving you a little insight into the Ireland that was and that may make you appreciate better the kind of life you enjoy today. Thank you for listening to me for so long.

The leader of the School pupils, Sandy R. Graper, then thanked Matilda for her thoughts before adjourning for some coke, chips and finger food.

School children today have no idea how hard school was in the past. Then, children had to walk to school but there was less traffic on the roads. Today, they travel in buses and cars. Pencils, pens, ink and copybooks or jotters were all that they had. Nowadays, they have computers, I-Pads, I-Phones, Smart-Phones and more. School work was hard and serious and corporal punishment existed. Today, it is a much more enjoyable experience and more child-centred.

Dancing at the Crossroads (1835) Trevor Thomas Fowler © N.U.I Galway

Grumpeen FM – Voice of the Local People

For a long time now, the inhabitants of the parish of Grumpeen have been campaigning for a Community Radio Station. Collections were held to gather some finance to make the project a reality. In addition, concerts, bingo sessions, card games, raffles and other events were also held in order to boost finances.

Once the finance was put in place, a site was procured and planning permission was obtained, after the plan of the building was drafted. Building took six months and when the new structure was completed, the local population seemed happy with the result.

In order to mark the official opening, the village of Grumpeen was decorated with bunting and colourful flags. Floral arrangements were put in place, including flower pots, containers and hanging baskets. A great atmosphere was created and the village looked beautiful. The local committee members were very pleased with the work done.

The Broadcasting Authority liked the new studios as they were all at ground level, with easy access to them, even for wheelchairs and people with disabilities. A frequency was allotted and the Station would be known as Grumpeen FM.

A small number of local people got some training in broadcasting and the

Schedule of Programmes was drawn up for the first month of the Station's life.

The next step was to fix a date for the official opening of the Station. It was decided by the Committee that some important figure should be invited to perform the opening and by unanimous vote, the person chosen was Professor Ollie Wishbone, D.Tech, D.Eng, D.Sc. from the University of Balderdash.

On the day of the opening, Professor Ollie stressed the importance of community enterprises and especially the need for communication technologies. He said that local radio was the voice of the people. He urged people to get involved in programme- making and he wished the station well.

With that, the station went live on air and all present at the opening ceremony, sat back and listened to the very first broadcast, entitled News of the Day. The following is the text of that inaugural programme:-

Welcome to you all, to our new Community Radio Station and to News of the Day. My name is Cilla Sophie Pincushion.

The wedding of Belinda Cricket and Josh Parrot did not happen on Friday. The groom stood up the bride. He changed his mind on the way to the church in Splintertown. He went off fishing instead with his mate Big Boots. The two hundred invited guests were left twirling their fingers. A riot broke out and the guards were called. They locked the mob up in the local hall, to cool off. Belinda was put on Valium.

The Pullet Towey has got her two hips done, of late. She is now up and running, a big change from her former condition. Mr. Squint McDermott said that she is moving well since she got her steel fitted.

Paudie Mike Luke is recovering at home after falling into a deep bog-hole over in Shismore and was nearly drowned. Jenny Diesel remarked that it was past time for him to be baptised, the pagan maggot.

The Crank Brady got his jaw broken and also two black eyes, during an altercation with Crab Feeney who has a tornado of a temper. The guards are investigating.

Julia Smutty fell off her antique bicycle on the road to Clooneydrip. A greyhound dashed across the road and sent her flying off her machine, into the bushes. It is reported that she has broken both legs, in two places. It is unlikely that she will be back on wheels again for a long time.

Polly Bridie Pat's arthritis has worsened and her weight has increased to obesity levels. As a result, she has now decided to write to the Pope to see if he can sort her out. She maintains that he has a hot line to the Lord Himself and He can solve everything. She is a woman of Faith.

Professor Brokenbrain will deliver a Lecture, next week, on the subject of Stupidity. He is the senior authority on the subject, in the University of Hopscotch.

The magician, Caterpillar X. Crawley died on stage, suddenly, while performing a disappearing act. The audience did not know whether it was part of the act or not. All we know is that he is still dead.

Little Biddy Johnny Dick who backs horses, every day, had a bad week. The Bookie cleaned her out, so she is now on strong medication and not talking to anyone. We have heard that she has imparted a special blessing over the Bookie but owing to the nature of the language we cannot repeat it here.

We are happy to report that the marriage of the two senior citizens, Jodi Tiger Artway and Peggy Flapper Goldfinch took place in Slaughterville. It was a quiet affair as they were both in their eighties and had very up-market wheelchairs.

During the ceremony, they kept smiling at each other as they thought that they were at a bingo session. Fr. Tombolo, OAP Chaplain had to bring some clarity into the performance and a solo singer rendered *When We Were Young.* The honeymoon is being spent in the Virgin Islands where they hope to relocate. They got the Papal Blessing as the priest said that they will need it.

A light aircraft came down in the townland of Skulkbeg North, hitting a thatched cottage in which an old man was living. He escaped uninjured but the aircraft knocked the chimney off the house and smashed the roof badly.

The occupant, Gulliver Porterman thought that the end of the world was at hand and started to say the Rosary. He is off his food since.

Finally, the visit of the circus Aquarius to the locality, recently was a great success. The children loved all the animals, great and small and kept feeding them goodies. The only downside was that a couple of the children got bitten by the snakes but they survived.

Snakes of a type are getting plentiful again, so St. Patrick would need to return to banish them as he did in the past.

The stars of the show were the clowns because they resembled the way people behave themselves, silly and outrageous, most of the time. Some of the children enquired as to whether they were politicians.

Spitting Liz was trying to climb over a fence with barbed wire recently and she had a mishap. Her skirt was ripped from top to bottom. Joe Smiler was in the field and he said afterwards that it must be the most attractive revelation since biblical times. The skirt was a write off and Liz is on tranquilisers.

A bunch of gurriers stole the ATM from outside the Bank of the Holy Spirit down in the town of Papamore. They were inspired to take it as they were badly in need of its contents, not the ATM. They dumped it in the nearby river and it was carried away.

That's all the news for now. This is Cilla Sophie Pincushion for Grumpeen FM signing off. Have a good day and keep your mind on your business. Bye!

The Beauty of the Bogland

In my travels of late I happened to call into a little shop in the countryside. I was taken by the name outside, over the door It read: "Goods for Nothing Here". I stupidly thought that that could mean what it said or perhaps, it just meant that prices were quite low and that there was value for money to be had.

In the shop that day was an individual, conversing with the shop owner and obviously enjoying the chatter. I felt that I should join them as I knew they were interesting characters. I soon found out that they were very different in their interests, so I asked to talk to the individual about his favourite interests or topics that he enjoyed reminiscing about.

The individual in question was Dinny. He was nicknamed The Cricket. His big thing was talking about the boglands because he lived right beside acres of lovely wild open heather-clad landscape. He told me that when he was young, the boglands were simply magic, a world of peace and joy. They were alive with people, amazing social places where turf was cut and saved.

Turf fires burned brightly while kettles hummed on top to make tea to go with lunches either taken with them to the bog or sometimes a family member or a wife would come with the lunch, riding on a bicycle.

Men who lived near the bog would get a signal from home that it was lunch-time. A family member would stand up on a height and wave a flag.

The bogs were a man's world and rarely would you see women working there in those times.

When lunchtime came, work would cease, sandwiches would be enjoyed with the tea and remember, there is no place quite like the bog for an appetite. The bogland air is fresh and exhilarating, perfumed by miles of heather, gorse and wild vegetation, ricks and clamps of turf.

With stomachs well filled, the men gathered into small groups, sat down on the heather and had a most wonderful conversation on all kinds of subjects. The local happenings would be sifted and any kind of scandal would be top of the charts. They spoke of fair days, tillage, prices, the Government, women, upcoming weddings, odd characters in the area and much more.

When the talk got going, the laughter was out of this world and you could hear the loud outbursts as far away as New York. The yarns were spun with great frivolity and it was the men's way of relaxing from the labour of turf-cutting.

Nearby were donkeys and carts. The donkeys would be unyoked and tied by means of a rope to the cart and given a nice bundle of hay to eat. There were dogs there too, lying down lazily on the bog and often asleep. Sometimes they would come to life and have a great chase. If they saw a hare they would give chase too and even show an interest in the wild birds.

The boglands contained a good deal of wild-life and many people who know bogs will have often herd the various bogland birds emitting their sounds, some sad and lonely, others chirpy and happy, all adding to the atmosphere, flitting here and there.

Hares, foxes and rabbits were often in hiding and when disturbed they would make a run for it and suddenly vanish again, to avoid the chasing foe. Frogs leaped with great excitement in the muddy holes and streams where rushes, furze bushes and wild cotton stood smartly on the sod. The hum of bees, flitting flies and insects added music and buzz to the scene.

Cutting turf in the West of Ireland had a certain ritual about it. First of all, the turf bank had to be cleaned, that is, the top foot or so of bog had to be removed as it would be covered with heather and then the actual turf would be revealed. The turf was cut with a slane. For "Down Turf" there was a slane to suit and it was pushed down into the wet turf vertically. The "Breast Slane" was used for cutting what was called Breast Turf. This slane was used horizontally, pushed inwards into the wet turf.

The cut sods of turf would be thrown off the slane into the hands of a spreader who filled up a flat bottomed barrow with the sods and then wheeled it out and emptied the barrow, leaving the cut sods in a small pile or heap.

When it got a bit of a skin it would be scattered out to dry properly. When reasonably hard it would be footed, that is, put standing up in very small clamps called grogeens. When dry, they would either be taken home in donkey, pony or horse cart to be stored for the Winter or taken out from the bank and left in a heap on the nearby road for removal by a tractor and trailer, or by horse and cart.

It would then be taken home and made into a rick near the house or perhaps put into a shed.

In a good dry year the turf used to be cut early, maybe in April, May or June so as to get a good chance to dry well. If the year was wet, there was far more work with the turf. It would be hard to get it dry and the bog itself would be very wet. If the ground was very bad, the turf might have to be left in the bog for the Winter, in big ricks, either on the bog or along a bog road nearby. Sometimes, the turf would have to be taken out in carts to the roadside or even put in bags and carried out which was laborious.

There were two kinds of turf. Stone turf was the best quality. It was black in colour and gave off good heat, but it could not stand too much good weather as it used to fall asunder. The brown turf was more robust and could stand up to any amount of dryness, but the quality was not that good and the heat output was less than from the stone turf.

The bogs of the West do not have great depth of turf as they are blanket bogs and many of them are now cut away but other usage is now possible in some places. They have been drained, reclaimed and planted with various types of vegetation.

Today many of the much frequented bogs of the past are empty and deserted and in ways, are now lonely desolate places. New types of fuels and heating systems have taken over as have smokeless products which are more beneficial to the environment, but fuel prices are quite high.

While this is so, there has been some return to the boglands in recent years when turf-cutters in some areas ran into trouble with the powers that be, such as the EU, over bog preservation. It is easy to see why farmers would be angry as their rights to cut turf have existed long before the EU was born. It is fine to conserve a certain amount of bogland, but after that, there would still be plenty left for the small number who still want to cut turf on their plots and their fuel costs for a year would be less.

In many bogland areas the old way of cutting turf has ceased and the turf-cutting machines have taken over, especially on the bigger, drier bogs but still, all the other chores connected with saving turf remain.

I enjoyed talking to Dinny, The Cricket, who gave me a great account of his recollections on the boglands and He finished up with a little verse:

"Yes, the bog-lands were just magic,
Where the workers all got tans.
Come back to hear the curlews,
And bring your kettles and your cans".

Ding and Dong and the Klondyke Gold

I was in a pub recently and I heard a couple of men talking about a great storyteller known as Clocker McAdoo from a place by the name of Rigmarole.

I felt a strong urge to go and meet the said Clocker. Having consulted my Diary I found an empty slot, so I made a note regarding my intent to visit His Lordship.

The day I called to see him, he was planting vegetables in his garden and on seeing me, he asked me to sit down with him on a big seat that he had placed in a cosy corner of his plot. We chatted and then I told him what my business with him was. Without further adoo, he launched into his choice of story, to soothe my curiosity.

A long time ago there were two brothers living here in this place and they were twins. The local people referred to them as Ding and Dong.

They were very interested in money but they had no jobs. They decided to emigrate to another country and the country they chose was Canada and they ended up in the Klondyke. It was famous for gold mining but it was very remote and conditions there were horrific. Life was tough but they got work from Prospectors who often did not work themselves. It was probably better than hanging around idle at home.

Despite the hardship they stayed, persevered and struggled on but felt that they should not be exploited, as they often were, and that they should try to put a bit of gold away for the rainy day, while they had the chance. This might mean, being a bit dishonest and it could be risky.

They had a considerable amount of the precious metal, so they decided that it might be wise to organise a way to get it back home to Rigmarole, without detection.

In the Klondyke there was a guy by the name of Dusty Busty who used to help miners to smuggle gold out of the area. For this he demanded a big reward for himself but it seems that he was expert at this kind of operation.

Ding and Dong met him in a Dance Club and he agreed to help them, for a price. A contract was signed and he told them that the gold they had would be moved out of the area, in small amounts, in suitcases, over a period, taking many months. He said that he would keep them informed as to how things would be progressing.

After some weeks, they were told that some of the gold was on its way home and should arrive, before long. As soon as all of it had arrived, it would be put into a large iron box and delivered to a designated place in Rigmarole.

Ding and Dong told Dusty Busty that as there was not any place in Rigmarole to which it could be delivered, the box would have to be hidden somewhere until such time as they could go home to claim it. Dusty said that that was not a problem as he had his assistant in Ireland who would take care of it for them. His name was Misery Mac.

When all the small consignments of gold had eventually arrived in Ireland and had been put together in a big iron box, Misery Mac transported it along a quiet country road, in the direction of Rigmarole.

He kept going until he came to a mountain area known as Ardnaclop. He knew where there was a big concealed cave, so he hid the iron box with its treasure there. He then closed the entrance with rocks and vegetation so that everything there looked normal and natural. While he was working on the entrance, a battered –looking vehicle came along the road and drove slowly past.

All of this action took place at 2.00 a.m. on a Thursday night which was very frosty and icy. The road was extremely dangerous and when Misery Mac was returning home, his vehicle skidded, at a bad bend, went over a stone wall and down hundreds of feet into a valley and he was killed. This was serious because, now, no one knew exactly where the gold was hidden.

Dusty Busty, in Canada, had a general idea of where it might be but had no exact details. When Dusty Busty learned of his assistant's tragic end in Ireland, he told the brothers, Ding and Dong about the disaster. They were shocked and decided to return home to see if they could find the gold. All they knew was that it was somewhere in the Ardnaclop mountains. They packed their bags and left The Klondyke as quickly as they could, in a very unhappy state. After some days they were back in Rigmarole and set to work to try and locate the treasure.

They said nothing to anyone but combed the mountains on their own. They had no great knowledge of the area but they found nothing.

In desperation they asked a Geographer from the College in Peachville to help. He took them through several features and along the road travelled by Misery Mac and eventually came to the Cave where he had hidden the gold, but, alas, there was nothing there. It was empty and the entrance was very visible when they approached it.

Ding and Dong were shattered as all their plans had come to nothing, in the end. They settled down in their old homestead, now in a state of disrepair.

Their health was not in great shape, and how could it be, after all the hardship in the Klondyke. These twin bachelors could now, at least, enjoy a well-earned rest, but with much less riches than they had hoped for.

The moral of the story seems to be that being dishonest does not seem to be a good way in which to set about doing one's business.

Regarding the iron box of gold, it is likely that the passer-by in the vehicle was tracking Misery Mac and probably knew the kind of business in which he was involved. The person in question may now be sipping quality wine, on a sunny beach in Australia, with no money worries.

Yes, I nearly forgot to tell ye why the pair were called Ding and Dong. They both had been sacristans in their local Church of Ireland and they took turns ringing the beautiful bells which were installed in the Church tower. It was hard work, not quite as hard as the slog in the Klondyke, but it did entail pulling heavy ropes down and letting them back up for several minutes, on a regular basis. The positive spin off was probably the toning of the muscles.

Pixie – Priscilla Pinktwit

I want to introduce you to a lady who lives out her days in a place called Ballyskitter. This quaint village is on the edge of a vast area of bogland which has a natural beauty of its own.

Pixie loves to go for long walks through the heather-clad wilderness, listening to the wild birds call and singing to herself, plucking an odd wild flower as she goes. The boglands are not that safe now as they are soft underfoot, not having been drained for years. There are many wide pools of water, overgrown with vegetation, numerous bogland plants and then there are deep bogholes also, filled with the acidic water of the area.

One day Pixie was strolling along on top of a high bank, probably day-dreaming and she forgot her business or so it seems. She wasn't the type that would depend on a Sat. Nav. In any event, she lost her balance and landed in the middle of a soft swamp. It was very muddy so, doubtless, she got her unexpected mud bath. At once, realising where she was, she recited a Litany but it was her own composition. It is not possible to put in print for reasons best known to the writer.

She started to scream for help and, luckily, she was heard by a man cutting rushes nearby who ran to her rescue. He threw her a rope and then pulled her slowly out of the swamp, bodily. She was perished with the cold and shivering. She was covered with mud from head to toe.

Her rescuer was a young fellow from the village of Stranglemore who was nicknamed Samson, known locally for his great sturdiness and strength.

He knew Pixie well. In fact it was he who christened her "Pixie" because when out and about she always wore a pixie. He believed that it suited her, down to the ground. Her real name is Priscilla Pinktwit and her people came from the village of Tullinafrack. She is what the locals call "One on the Shelf". She never married because she was as particular as hell.

Where men were concerned, she thought that she could get her prescription filled by simply listing out her priorities such as size, shape, height, looks, hobbies and brain power. Alas! No suitable guy, ticking all the boxes on her list, ever showed up. As Grumpy Grady put it: *The lads must not have fancied the mountainous scenery or maybe it was just the space she occupied. Shed load, I would say, shed load and economise on the fuel!*

Pixie is now doing her best to lose weight but she is plagued by her awful big appetite. In her own words, there is no day that she would not have two dinners with large portions, a couple of goes at lunch, a big supper and lots of snacks. She adores chips, fat bacon, soft drinks and loads of sugar and salt. She is expert at clocking up the calories, a great candidate for Operation Transformation.

Her nearest neighbour, Foxie, has nice words to describe Pixie. She says that she is bulging out all over and is ready for the factory any day now.

Apart from the food, Pixie does not spend much money on other things such as make-up, cosmetics of any kind or luxuries. She is plain-living. She comes Nature's Way, natural and unspoiled.

One thing can be said in her favour. She is very generous with Charities and likes to help people in need. She is well healed because a brother of her's was involved in business in Chicago, Illinois and he left all his money to Pixie in his Will. She now uses it wisely.

She has recently taken her weight problem in hand and has employed a PE Instructor to sort her out, so it is all stretching, hopping, jumping, moving, pressing up, pressing down, standing, sitting, jogging, walking, running, pushing, shoving and even dancing.

A neighbouring young fellow has recently taken an interest in her. When he passes her by on the road, he smiles and throws out some fancy chat and she looks at him and continues on walking.

She goes slowly but he walks fast and on his return, he meets her again. He smiles and utters some words, looks at her and moves on. All the exercise she is into now is beginning to turn heads and results could follow.

In no time now, the model figure will emerge and Pixie will eventually be the pride and queen of Ballyskitter. Then she can take a bow, maybe get a man and live happily ever after.

Pixie, of course, has more than a weight problem on her hands. Before it leaves my head, I had better tell you something about her other headache.

Some time ago, she awoke one morning and saw an old red van pulling up on the road in front of her residence. She thought that she was just imagining things, but no, without delay, she saw a very ungroomed filthy looking guy walking in towards her front door.

His hair was like a forest and his beard was long and looked dirty. He was dressed in old worn clothes and his shoes resembled a sinking ship. Pixie was wondering who he was and what could be his business.

She had little time to think. Could he be a conman? Could he be a criminal? Maybe he is selling something? Maybe he will rob and kill me.

There was a knock on the door. Reluctantly, she opened the door slowly and observed her visitor close up, in all his misery. She was armed with a big long piece of a shovel handle, just in case of an attack.

Pixie picked up enough courage to ask him who he was and why had he called. He replied – *Good morning, Priscilla. My name is William Aloysius. I live twelve miles from here in an old caravan. I am not long there. Before that I was in a derelict house in the village of Pollnaheehaw.*

You may not know that my mother and your mother is one and the same person. Did you not know that? Perhaps, she never told you or any family member that I was around before the lot of ye. Your mother is now dead, so you cannot ask her about me. When the couple that adopted me died, I fell by the wayside.

She listened carefully to what he said and then told him that he must be talking to the wrong family, that her mother would have mentioned him, down the years. With that she closed the door and William Aloysius made his way back to his van.

Priscilla was troubled and did not know whether to believe him or not. She hesitated for a few minutes and then made up her mind to check out his credentials.

She walked down the village to the local historian, Billy Paddy Andy and put him the question re William Aloysius. He had no trouble confirming his identity and filled her in on everything. He said that he had met him a few times over in Glenfeckin Lower in a pub called the Porter Jar.

At the heel of the hunt, Priscilla was happy to know that the caller was genuine but she was sad that he was in such a bad state. She blamed her late mother for being so secretive with her and the entire family, but, in the past, things were just put under the carpet and left there.

As Priscilla was well off herself, she took pity on poor broken William and decided to give him an upgrade. Her grandfather had left her a nice old world cottage in the village of Skelpnahoo.

She tracked him down and signed over the cottage to him in the solicitors office which was run by Eddie Claws McRuff. She also wrote him a big fat cheque and told him to go and buy himself some good clothes and food and smarten himself up.

You see, there was generosity in her, Irish style and she had a good soft heart. The poor man fell on his knees and thanked her for her kindness.

She told Billy Paddy Andy what she had done and he was impressed. Then he said: *You know, Priscilla, it is a more blessed thing to give than to receive, especially when the need to help is great. Well done, woman, well done!*

The moral of this story is that when an opportunity arises to be charitable, helpful and supportive, it is right to respond in a positive way. That is what the Lord would want us to do. Well done, Pixie!.

The Pilgrim Faith of Knock – Cnoc Mhuire

One day, not so long ago, I met Paddy the Rasher Muldoon and he said to me *You go around talking to people and asking them to tell you stories. You should go up to Slievenamuck and talk to John Joe Ned Nerney and his wife, Florrie Jane. They are great talkers and also very religious people, good on Church matters.*

I took Paddy's advice and did the trip to Slievenamuck. When I arrived at their cottage, John Joe was washing potatoes in a bucket and Florrie was doing the dishes. I got a welcome and the chores ceased. I apologised for disrupting the work as I knew that they must have a daily routine like the rest of us.

Florrie threw in the ball and began talking about the great Faith that Irish people had, in times past. Churches were packed with people. People received the Sacraments regularly. Priests were greatly respected and they exercised a firm discipline in society. There were many priests to cater for the people, in all parishes.

Vocations to the priesthood were numerous and there were families that gave two or three members to the priesthood and there might be two or three nuns from the same family as well. Families were big in the past, unlike today.

Parents encouraged their children to go on for service in the Church and there was an emphasis on prayer and the family Rosary in the homes.

In every kitchen, there were holy pictures of the Blessed Virgin Mary, the

Holy Family, the Sacred Heart of Jesus with a red light burning in front of it as well as pictures of the saints and the popes and even a Mass Rock scene.

In the Month of May, there would be a May Altar, with a statue or picture of Our Lady and seasonal flowers.

John Joe nodded his head in agreement and then picked up where Florrie left off.

The strong Faith of the Irish then was very much in evidence at holy places such as at ancient pilgrimage sites, holy wells and monastic centres, but where it was most easily observed was at the Shrine of Knock in Co. Mayo. There, the pilgrim Faith on Mary's Hill – Cnoc Mhuire – has continued to inspire and impress.

John Joe, now, ninety five years old, said that he used to visit Knock Shrine on the 14th August every year and remain on for the following day, the Feast of the Assumption of Mary – Lá Fhéile Muire sa bhFómhar.

There used to be an All-Night Vigil on the 14th August when pilgrims stayed up, all night, fasting and praying.

Many did the rounds of the Parish Church, barefooted and on their knees, praying the Rosary. There used to be a constant hum of prayer, broken only by the singing of hymns.

Many of the pilgrims would have walked from their homes in counties Mayo, Roscommon, Galway, Sligo and from more distant places, often on rough gravel roads.

Some would walk barefooted and most would carry sticks or canes. The Rosary would be recited on the way and they would attend Mass at 6.00 a.m. in Knock.

People living in houses, on the route to Knock, could hear the hum of prayer or maybe conversation as the pilgrims passed by.

Thousands of pilgrims were always present on the 15th August, to take part in the Mass and the ceremonies. The Sick were given pride of place and were cared for by nurses, doctors, Stewards and Handmaids of the Shrine.

The pilgrims would be walking around the Parish Church, anti-clockwise, performing the traditional Station. I was taken by the devotion and prayerfulness of the pilgrims.

The mix of languages was beautiful, the Irish speakers from Connemara, with their Rosaries, mingling with the English and other foreign languages.

The Connemara women wore big heavy colourful shawls and some, with wrinkled faces that reflected their years.

An image that stays with me is of a lone Connemara woman, in her shawl, praying on her knees at the Shrine Gable, completely oblivious to the thousands around her, reciting An Phaidrín (The Rosary) as Gaeilge (In Irish).

Every year, on the 15th August a large contingent of travellers was present. They came to the Shrine in carts drawn by horses, for many years but later they acquired vans, cars and caravans.

When they became motorised, they came in much greater numbers, sometimes in long processions. The Gardaí had then to regulate and control their movements on the roads and to see that they parked their vehicles correctly.

Pilgrims did not like to see too many of them around as they could start begging and cause annoyance, if not checked.

Travellers did not like to be restricted and when restrictions were introduced their numbers decreased greatly.

The older traveller women wore shawls and were often carrying babies in their arms. The young traveller women were dressed in modern style, sometimes scantily. They used to parade, up and down, in an effort to attract the attention of the young traveller men, with a view to marriage.

Another eye-catching scene was that of the numerous priests spaced all over the grounds in front of the Shrine, hearing Confessions in the open. It was, at once, both inspiring and impressive.

The Irish people always had a great devotion to Our Lady's Assumption long before it was defined a Dogma of the Church in 1950.

When Our Lady appeared in Knock on the 21st August, 1879, she had, on her head, a large and beautiful crown which presupposed her Assumption into Heaven, body and soul, because she was sinless, immaculate. Following this, she was crowned Queen of Heaven and Earth.

It is because of her Immaculate Conception that her Assumption takes place. Both are complementary Dogmas.

Florrie was anxious to add a bit more to the recollections, so John Joe gave her a nod to begin and with that, the ninety year old, took off.

She said that she remembers hearing of people who were healed or cured at Knock, a blind man getting his sight back, a paralytic on a stretcher standing up and walking, one cured of cancer and another cured of T.B.

She was very interested in the modes of transport that the pilgrims depended upon to get to Knock. Bicycles were parked everywhere along the main street. There were ponies and traps, horses and sidecars, donkeys and carts, some old-fashioned buses, vans and small motor cars.

The village of Knock, back in the thirties and forties was small and undeveloped. The Church and Shrine were the main features, around which were areas of grass.

There were some small thatched cottages along the main street, the presbytery, a convent, a school, a few small shops and some stalls selling souvenirs.

There was a thatched cottage, also, to the East of the Church where some of the Knock visionaries lived, in their day.

I believe there were fifteen official witnesses to the Apparition and they included men, women, teenagers and children ranging in age from six years to seventy four.

It must have been a wonderful experience for those people looking at the Heavenly Scene, at the south Gable of the parish Church, in a brilliant light as the raindrops fell upon them, in the darkness of the night- Our Lady, St. Joseph, St. John the Apostle, the Altar, the Lamb, the Cross and the Angels.

It is clear from what the witnesses saw, that Knock was meant to be, not just a Marian shrine but also a Eucharistic shrine. Ireland's people always had a great devotion to the Eucharist, the Mass, for example, during the Penal Days and also before and after.

Florrie concluded her offering and then John Joe gave me his parting shot. He cleared his throat and said – *I will tell you something. We, Irish, are very slow to deal with important matters.*

We have many candidates for sainthood but no pressure is brought to bear on the powers that be. When the late Pope John Paul II (now a saint) visited Ireland in 1879 he said "You Irish are careless about your saints". I believe that the witnesses of Knock are already saints. Heaven held nothing against them.

As John Joe's contribution was ending, Florrie had a cup of tea ready accompanied by a rich homemade sweet-cake with icing on top. At that point, it was badly needed to refresh the body.

I put one final question to Florrie Jane. I asked her could she tell me what Knock Apparition tells us. She reflected for a moment and then said:-

The Apparition itself is the message. Its silent symbolism speaks to us if we look at it and reflect upon it for a while. Everything in it has a meaning and message.

It tells us that Heaven exists; that Christ has redeemed and saved us; that He is risen from the dead and is now in glory, adored by the Angels; that he has left us the Mass, the Eucharist, the gift of Himself in Holy Communion.

It tells us that the Blessed Virgin Mary is Queen of Heaven and Earth. She is our spiritual Mother who prays and intercedes for us, cares about us and is concerned about our welfare.

Mary's Golden Rose, in full bloom, tells us much about her. It is the greatest symbol there is of love, her love for Jesus and for all of us. It is the symbol of her Rosary, of her Immaculate Conception, of her mystical nature. She is the Mystical Rose of God. It is the symbol of the fullness of her charisms and of her beauty. Through the ages, she has been referred to as the Rose of Sharon, Jericho's Rose.

It tells us that the saints are praying for us in Heaven, St. Joseph guarding, guiding and protecting us on our life's journey, the layman, worker, with whom we can identify; St. John confronts us with the book of Scriptures – the Word of God – to ponder on, to live by and to be loyal to it.

As I left for home, I felt that I had been in University for, at least, a few hours. I got a taste of theology and more, so it was time well spent in Slievenamuck.

I reflected on all that was said and must say now myself, that Knock of the first half of the twentieth century was very unlike the Knock of today with its new Shrine, chapels, buildings, offices, great Basilica, shopping malls, parking areas and an International Airport.

Pope John Paul II (now a saint) and Pope Francis have come as pilgrims and many other famous people such as Mother Teresa of Calcutta (now a saint), Fr. Patrick Peyton, C.S.C. (on the road to sainthood) and more.

The shrine's first Custodian was Archbishop John Mac Hale of Tuam. It was he who gave it approval in the Spring of 1880.

He chose his words well when he said in his Statement to the Press of his day – *"It is a great blessing for the poor people of the West, in their wretchedness, misery and suffering that the Blessed Virgin Mother of God has appeared among them".*

Florrie Jane's remark that Knock Shrine should be both a Marian and Eucharistic Shrine has been endorsed by the Vatican. As I write, Pope Francis has just officially announced the recognition of Knock as an International Eucharistic and Marian Shrine, at the request of the Pontifical Council for the New Evangelisation.

Andy the Anvil on Trades Old and New

One of the areas of Interest that I had growing up and which I still have is what I term THE TRADES. It could well happen that you might also have an interest in those same things. If so, that is wonderful.

In the older Ireland tradesmen could be found all over the country, in towns and villages. Back then many of the things that people needed badly could not be got in shops or other outlets. That is why tradesmen were so necessary. They were able to make and do what people required from time to time.

I knew a man down in the village of Mucklawn who could tell me a few things about trades and tradesmen. He was Andy the Anvil Delaney. He was a backsmith himself but is now retired. He worked in a big forge with a very wide entrance because he used to put shoes on big horses, ponies and donkeys hoofs also.

Farmers kept those animals then, for farm work such as ploughing and for drawing carts and other equipment.

A big coal fire always burned in the forge perched high up on a stone structure and a big strong bellows fanned the fire into a bright red hot inferno. It was the coal fire that caused the interior walls of the forge to be black and dusty.

This was necessary as the smith needed the heat to soften and shape the iron for the animal's shoes. This he did on the anvil with a heavy hammer. Using a long-handled tongs, he would then dip the shoes into a trough of water to cool them.

He would size each shoe to fit the hoofs, attach them with long nails and then rasp the hoofs to give a finished look.

Blacksmiths were often big, tall, strong men because they needed strength when dealing with big strong animals. Andy the Anvil had these proportions in plenty.

In his forge as in many others there was a huge collection of tools of every kind, large and small and unusual. In some cases they were handed down from father to son and more.

As time went on tractors replaced horses and other animals on the farm and mechanisation became the in thing. As a result, the importance of the forge dwindled and there was less work for blacksmiths. Over time, both forges and blacksmiths became things of the past. Some of the old forges are still standing idle and decaying with their often thatched roofs falling in.

Andy then told me that there were many different tradesmen in the various villages around but in time, they all, too, disappeared.

The shoemaker, also referred to as the Cobbler, was essential in the days when life was simple and people were not well off. A pair of new shoes had to last a long time, so when repairs were needed the shoemaker was there to put on new soles and heels and stitch footwear that might be torn also.

He worked with a small iron object which was heavy and solid and it was known as the LAST. It was on it that the shoe was placed, upside down, when being repaired.

When mass production of shoes began and there was a growth in shoe shops and in big stores, prices reduced and Sales became common. Bargains could be had and people had more money in their pockets.

These new developments led to the demise of the shoemakers and remember, there could be an entire family, maybe, three or four brothers, all shoemakers, working in the same premises.

Andy Delaney then referred to a big number of other trades that he knew of but that also have vanished from the scene, all because of manufacturing output and big supplies of everything, coming into the country. Readymade items replaced the handmade items.

His list included tailors, coopers, saddlers, carpenters, stonemasons, thatchers, basket-makers, tinsmiths and many more.

In the past, the trades were a man's world as women did not get involved in them. They were homemakers and reared families.

Some women went into service or worked as sales' ladies in shops. Others became carers or nurses. Not a few were spinners of wool and linen cloth for yarn, using the distaff and spindle. Many of them, too, emigrated to America,. England and elsewhere.

There were those who carried on cottage industries at home such as arts and crafts, made jams and butter and kept poultry. They sold eggs on the small farms to the local shopkeepers, and butter also.

Today, women have become involved in all aspects of modern life, including politics and have qualified in all the professions as doctors, therapists, pharmacists, architects, teachers, technicians, engineers, lawyers and many more.

As regards the trades, women are now replacing the men's trades with others. They are taking up apprenticeships in mechanics, welding, construction, technology, aviation, stone-craft, stonemasonry, energy, electrics, transport, plumbing, engineering and so on.

These trends are encouraging as they will make for a better gender balance for the future and more equality.

After all that serious talk from Andy, he asked me did I know anything about the horseshoe or what it is supposed to do. I told him that I knew nothing about it.

With that he burst into chatter and said that it dates back a very long time when a blacksmith had dealings with the Devil.

In England, there was a blacksmith who became a saint known as St. Dunstan. One day, he put a shoe on a horse and unknown to him, the horse happened to be the Devil. The shoe caused the Devil much pain and suffering.

Dunstan made a deal with the Devil. He said that he would remove the shoe if he promised never to enter a house with a horseshoe.

It is said that this is how the horseshoe became a symbol of protection and good luck. Many believe that if placed in a house, it can bring health, happiness and prosperity and also keep evil away.

Andy then went on to give me some information on St. Dunstan. He was born in the year 909 A.D. and was educated by Irish monks. He became a monk himself and was ordained in 943 A.D.

Later on, he was appointed as the first Abbot of Glastonbury Abbey, only a few miles from where he was born. After that he was appointed bishop of Worcester, then bishop of London and lastly, as Archbishop of Canterbury in 959 A.D.

He died in the year 988 A.D. and was buried in Canterbury cathedral.

He restored monastic life to England and also reformed the English Church. There are many stories of his greatness and popularity.

He was canonised by Pope Alexander III in 1029 A.D.

St. Dunstan is the patron saint of blacksmiths and all kinds of smiths such as locksmiths, goldsmiths, silversmiths and also of musicians and bell ringers.

He is venerated in the Roman Catholic Church, the Eastern Orthodox

Church and also in the Anglican Communion.

Andy pointed out to me that Canterbury was Roman Catholic until the Reformation in the 16th century and thereafter, it was Anglican.

Glastonbury Abbey now lies in ruins and the original Canterbury cathedral dates back to the year 597A.D. It was founded by Augustine, later St. Augustine. He had been sent to England by Pope Gregory the Great with a group of missionaries to convert the Anglo-Saxons to Christianity.

It was replaced by a new structure in the year 1070 A.D. and altered again in the year 1834 A.D.

I thanked my good friend Andy for all his recollections and information and gave him the price of a few drinks.

Then he popped into his house and emerged again, very quickly, with a lovely horseshoe in his hand. He then said *That's for you to take home and hang up in your house where it can be seen. Then, you can tell the Devil to get lost.*

At least, that is what I think he said.

Mary Majella on Sunday Mass, Mischief and Mission

Many people speak about Mary Majella Milldew with great affection as she has a wonderful memory of times past and she loves recalling them, not that the sun shone then all the time or that life was easy.

Her favourite topic is talking about Sunday, as it used to be. Back then, attendance at Mass was the highlight of the day. The Mass was celebrated in Latin and many people knew the Latin off by heart – "Introibo ad altare Dei, ad Deum qui laetificat juventutem meam". The priest had his back to the congregation and the altar servers were boys.

Everything revolved around Mass and everyone had to attend on Sundays. There was no such thing as not attending. If anyone of the young brigade objected, a telling off would follow and sometimes a belt across the face might put one flying in under the kitchen table. The parents called the shots. They were in control.

The previous day or evening before, all were expected to go to Confession and again, no excuses were accepted. You had also to keep the strict fasting rules and people did not question them. Queues of penitents were a common sight in the churches on Saturdays when there would be several hours of Confessions. There were far more priests hearing Confessions in the parishes then, unlike today and a greater attachment to that sacrament also.

Penances handed out by priests were often not easy for people, if you had anything major to tell. Molly Mary said that she heard a poor man say that he was told to climb Croagh Patrick three times in his bare feet and not to drink any alcohol in the process.

A local man who heard the story wanted to know was he Al Capone and how many murders had he committed.

Before going to bed on the Saturday night, all the household had to wash and scrub themselves thoroughly and arrange their clothes for the Sunday morning.

Those were the days when there was no such thing as Vigil Masses on Saturday evenings or on the Eve of church holydays.

Everyone in the family had to kneel down and recite the Rosary before going to bed, trimmings included.

On rising in the morning, people dressed up very well. The men put on their best suits, commonly referred to as their Sunday suits and they were very likely the only good suits they had. Collars and ties were worn as were hats and caps. Shoes were well polished, faces were well shaved and the hair was short and tidy.

In the church, the men sat on one side and the women on the other as if both sides had a falling out before Mass. This same procedure operated in many other situations as well.

Sunday was a day of rest and it was well observed. Shopping was not on the agenda because shops of any size were closed.

Parishes had Sodalities or Guilds with Leaders or Heads as they were called and Children of Mary groups were common.

At certain times such as after Christmas and Easter, the priests used to read out the Lists of subscriptions that parishioners gave and there was usually much comment afterwards.

Johnny Giblets didn't overdo it, but then he is known for his meanness. Bullock Henderson, with all his wealth gave nothing. He will leave it all after him. Biddy Flushing dug deep. She has shamed the rest of us.

In those days contributions could be very small, many just five or ten shillings, in the old currency, as money was a scarce commodity.

Occasionally, the silence of the church would be disturbed during Mass, usually during the Sermon. One Sunday the priest was speaking about the importance of communication between people, and it seems that two fellows, down on one knee, at the back of the church, just inside the entrance, with caps resting on the other, decided to put his message into practice.

They were talking loudly and could be heard over a wide areas of the church. They were obviously making a bargain for cattle. One of them said – *I like the heifers and I have offered you a decent price. Will you give them to me for that and I will give you a good luck penny. Don't break my ruling.*

The other fellow replies – *You will have to go higher. They are prize-winning animals.*

The response came quickly – *That may be so but it seems that your dogs have eaten the tails off them. They are trimmers.*

With that, the priest stopped talking and referred to the commotion at the back of the church. He said that he could not compete with the opposition. He asked those responsible to quit or leave the church. A stunning silence gripped the place and necks were strained, turning around to see could they identify the culprits.

It was the women, however, that stole the limelight, in their lovely costumes and blouses, and if the weather was inclement, they wore long coats. Their crowning glory was their headgear, gorgeous hats with plumes, decorations and multiple shapes. In those bygone days, all women wore hats in church.

After Mass, as people met and carried on conversation outside, one could hear some comments on the women's style – *Did ye notice the Crilly pair – Pinky and Perky - parading up the church to the front row of seats, show-offs, herself leading the way and the head up in the air and himself, trailing behind her, dragging his feet as if walking on ice. They could have slipped into the side aisle unnoticed but that would not be Pinky's form at all.*

After the chatter outside the church, some would go to a small local shop and buy a newspaper and maybe a few groceries before returning home. Some would walk and others had bicycles. A small number had traps or sidecars drawn by ponies or horses. Baby Ford cars were a novelty then.

The afternoons were quiet and relaxed. After dinner which was always in the early afternoon, adults might listen to a football match on the radio, but not every house had one.

Some country people kept greyhounds and they often went hunting for hares and rabbits in the boglands.

Others had guns and they used to go out shooting wildlife.

Fishing in the small lakes and ponds was popular with both young and old.

Ball-alleys were common and handball was an important sport. People were happy with simple pastimes, some years ago.

Papers would be read and the youngsters might kick a football around, in a local field or go for a spin on a bicycle to meet friends or pals. Planning would take place for the evening and night, for some social activity.

In rural areas there was not much social life. Adults played cards or went to pubs for a drink where the local gossip was entertaining.

Musicians and singers often performed in people's houses and even danced in the kitchens and even out in the fresh air at the crossroads.

There were some small dance halls, here and there but there was nothing fancy about them. They were usually family owned and run. The bands playing in them were made up of local people. That is the way things were before the coming of the big ballrooms and the elaborate showbands.

Many young people and some not so young, found love and romance in the small old halls. Alcohol was not allowed in them but the better ones might have a mineral bar and cloakrooms.

In the dancing area, the men assembled on one side of the hall and the women stood on the other side. Segregation was the usual set-up. They resembled opposing armies waiting to strike, in what one could call the battle for hearts.

Conversation during the dances was possible because the bands were not like the high-powered showbands of a later time that were so loud that conversation was rarely possible.

The chit-chat would go something like this, the man leading: *Do you come here often? What do you think of the talent tonight? Are you a local or have you travelled here? Do you like the band? Would you like an orange or a lemonade? Will you keep the next dance for me? Can I see you to your bike when the dance is over or can I walk you home?*

The questioning paid dividends sometimes and success could have been achieved that might lead on to greater things at a later date. It must be said, that many good marriages were triggered in those less than glamourous settings.

Molly Mary recalled some of the pranks youngsters used to carry out on the nights of dances. They would get together in a group and plan things to do. They used to come to the halls and look in through the windows at the dancers.

She related how a group got together over in the village of Gugeen Upper on the night of a dance and played havoc. Many of the dancers had come to the dance on bicycles. They put a ladder up to a flat roof of a building attached to the hall and then some of them passed the bicycles up to guys on the ladder and the roof and stood them up in lines. They then removed the ladder, hid it and scrammed.

Later the same night they found a small car unlocked, as nobody locked anything at that time. They entered it and turned on all the lights in order to flatten the battery. They moved on then to another car and removed the two front wheels but left them beside the car. Lastly, they let the air out of all the tyres of another vehicle.

Tempers were frayed after the dance and some homework had to be executed before being able to go home. To make things worse the night was very bad and the rain was bucketing down on the mayhem scene.

To round off the night, the group raided a nearby orchard and went home with the makings of juicy apple tarts that could last for weeks. The ringleader of the group ended up in prison later for robbing an old man in the village of Glosstown. His nickname was Big Nose Brannigan.

Molly Mary recalled another regularly recurring event of bygone days, namely, the Parish Mission which could have a full week for the men and another full week for the women.

She referred to a Mission held in the church of St. Michael the Archangel down in Cloondude. Six tall missioners arrived to give it. It turned out to be a very scary occasion, so much so that many of the young people present were crying and frightened.

The cause of the stress and fear was the Sermons that were preached. Most of the talk was about hell and the Devil, the fire of Hell, the demons of Hell, the nature of Hell. The church seemed to be on fire itself and people imagined that they could see flames rising up that would engulf everyone. The tempest of words continued for a long time and when the Sermons ended, things relaxed a bit.

I can tell you that no sin was committed in Cloondude at that time or for a long time after. The fear of God was instilled in everyone or should I say the fear of the Devil himself. Those were the days of fire, fear and brimstone. There was no mention of God, the loving, caring, forgiving father of all. The prodigal son would not have had a chance at all in Cloondude.

The local comedian was asked did he know who gave the Mission. He hesitated for a moment and said: *As far as I know, they are referred to as the Firemen.*

I hope that Mary Majella lives another while to keep us informed that life in the past in Ireland was not quite the same as life today. God bless you! Keep talking, for you have the gift of the gab.

Memories of Springtime with Billy Eddie Jack

On one of my travels recently, I found myself in a quaint old-world village with many neat well-kept thatched cottages. It had a real Gaelic name and it was Cnocnacoille which translates as the hill of the wood. It has a hill to be sure and there is a wood on its south side.

I met a man in the local shop run by a pleasant chatty specimen of the human species. I speak of none other than Biddy Bridle. The man in question was Billy Eddie Jack McGoofey.

He told me that he never carries a watch or wears such a thing as he does not like being under any time restraint. He said that when God made time, he made plenty of it. He at once gave me a lecture on people he knew who all died very young because of their lifestyle. They never relaxed, never sat down, never took a break, never took a holiday, running and racing all the time, from Billy to Jack and back again. They ate their dinner standing up and it is no wonder that they often vomited it up again.

All of this was due to their eagerness to accumulate more and more money, greedy, grasping people with little regard for anyone. Well, I can tell you they all died of stress, anxiety, lack of sleep and a proper relaxed manner of living. The world is a better plac without that kind of animal.

I knew from what he was saying that he was in no hurry and seemed to me to be longing for a good conversation. We went outside and sat under a nice budding tree, on a backless seat.

The sight of the newly awakening tree was the hint for him to start talking about Spring. Nearby, were the year's first daffodils.

We all know from writers and poets that no Season is as beautiful as Spring. There are many reasons for that.

It is a season of new life, new growth, resurrection. It is a Season of hope and promise. It is a season of new beginnings. It makes us feel happy and it lifts the gloom. We feel that we have courage to continue on.

With the help of Billy Eddie Jack we may learn something of what Spring was like some years ago.

Spring he said, when he was young was very different to Spring today. The name is about all that is unchanged.

A good deal of tillage was done on small farms in the past. Today, there is very little with the result that one can hardly tell that it is Spring. The Season then began on St. Brigid's Day but not so nowadays.

In the past, farmers, on the small farms ploughed the land with a plough and a team of horses and good ploughing it was. At a later date, the arrival of the tractor put an end to that. Then the ploughed land would be scuffled and harrowed and seeds applied to produce cereal crops of oats, barley and wheat.

Harrowing would follow again and rolling in order to cover the seeds, to prevent birds from picking them up. All the work was manual and physical.

Some of the ploughed and harrowed land would be set aside for potatoes and vegetables. In it, drills would be formed with the plough and ridges also when the land was initially ploughed.

Farmyard manure which would have built up over the Winter would be applied to the drills and ridges and other crops before sowing the seeds, procured from local shops.

Some farmers would have their own seed potatoes from the previous year. The potatoes kept for seed would have to be slitted because large potatoes could be divided so as to make two or three slits. A good slit would have at least one eye or bud and often more than that.

When sown, they had to be covered with soil by the plough, in the case of drills or manually with a shovel, in the case of ridges. That was very hard work.

Farmyard manure had to be carted out to the lea land and spread there in order to ensure a good growth in the meadows and also in the land for grazing. Lime was put on land also and later, artificial manure in the form of fertilisers became available.

The slurry tanks did not exist then, thank God, as the whiff from them is much worse than the smell of farmyard manure.

Billy Eddie Jack then switched topic in order to tell me about the lovely gardens of vegetables that were to be seen in all the villages, usually quite near the houses. They were always beautifully kept, very neat without a weed in sight.

The gardens would have, potatoes, cabbage, onions, carrots, parsnips, beetroot, lettuce and much more. There was usually a forest of rhubarb.

As time went on and big stores developed, especially supermarkets, the vegetable gardens gradually disappeared as the big commercial operators were able to provide an abundance of vegetables and plenty of choice as well.

Billy Eddie then moved away from agriculture to a spiritual practice of Springtime, namely, the Stations.

In rural Ireland, especially and to a lesser degree in towns and cities, Mass was celebrated in people's homes in the Spring and again in the Autumn.

Every home was expected to facilitate this practice, unless there was some serious reason for not doing so.

A home in each village would be listed and for the next round of Stations, another home would be listed and that procedure would continue on until every house, in every village would have been involved.

If a village was large, with a big number of homes, it could take many years for the Stations to come around again. In small villages, homes would have the Stations more frequently.

When homes were listed for Stations, great activity began. Rural homes in times past, were often old and not well maintained like today, so much work was usually carried out to have them in good shape for the Stations.

There would be extensive painting of walls, inside and out. Windows and doors would be painted. Streets and pathways leading to the houses were cleaned and resurfaced. Money had to be spent to put everything in order.

That is why some people were reluctant to take the Stations because in those times, money was scarce. If any family had a problem, priests in some parishes were understanding and would agree to have the Mass celebrated in the local church instead.

Other priests were not happy with that and there were cases where the priest went to the refusing house, set up an altar outside the house, on the lawn or garden, if the weather was fine, and celebrated Mass there.

This kind of situation was rare enough but it could occur if there was only a bachelor in the house or if a person in the house was very old or incapacitated.

It could happen, too, if a house were in poor repair. Very rarely would it be a lack of Faith or an anti-church attitude.

In the past, the Station Mass was usually in the morning and the priest would arrive with a large wooden box containing all the requirements for celebrating Mass. They would be put in place and candles would be lighted on an altar that would have been erected, usually in the kitchen of the rural houses.

The officiating priest would begin by hearing Confession, then vest for

Mass and welcome the people from the village in question. The attendance was generally good. It was an opportunity for the priest to get to know the people.

Following the Mass, the priest or priests would have breakfast and it was always specially prepared. A popular item then was grapefruit.

When the priest or priests had gone, all the villagers were treated to breakfast and there could also be some alcohol available such as whiskey, port wine or sherry.

After some time, priests did not like the idea of having drink connected to the Station Mass, so it was decided to cut out the food and drink elements entirely and to provide just a cup of tea and a biscuit. Many places also moved the Station Mass from morning to evening.

The passage of time brings change and sadly, this lovely religious and community event has largely disappeared today. Some parishes have tried to preserve the Stations by facilitating those who would still like to have Mass in their homes. The number looking for this is now very small.

The reason for the decline may be due to a different mind-set on the part of the younger generation, a culture change. It may be due to a weaker Faith or indifference. The shortage of priests may be a factor also, priests now having extra work-loads compared to the past.

In the Ireland of today it would be very easy to have a Station Mass because of the excellent quality and grandeur of homes with every mod con and facilities.

Billy Eddie then digressed to relate a funny incident that occurred at the Stations in a neighbouring village by the name of Mullaghmaol. It seems that there must have been some last minute painting and varnishing of chairs and when the two ladies and a chap that were sitting on them stood up, they were a bit restrained.

The chairs were solidly attached to their posteriors and if the chairs could speak their words would be *Ye go ahead and we'll follow ye.*

With that, I felt that I had enough for one day and in any event, Billy Eddie Jack had to go home to feed his geese and ducks and pigs and other things. He felt, too, that he might get a telling off from his fiery wife, Hilda Honeycomb for his long delay in returning home.

You are right! You guessed it. Hilda is a beekeeper. That's why, according to Snooty Cunningham she is such a sweetie. She'll never be stung because she blows smoke from her cigarettes at them, all day long.

The Three Lovely Lassies of Lusheen

In the very compact village of Lusheen is where you may happen to bump into the three lovely lassies, physically acceptable but with different mind-sets. They are triplets and single as none of them ever met men to put a ring on their fingers.

They operate in their quaint little house as if it were a Republic. Each one is responsible for one or more areas of work or a department, just like the Government.

Molly is minister for food, drinks, shopping and finance. She decides what the weekly budget will be and how much can be spent on groceries and bills. She keeps a close eye on everything and sometimes she introduces cutbacks in order to keep the books balanced. This move is not usually applauded by the two sisters but they go along with it, in the hope that the following week may be better.

Molly shops once a week in the local small shop and as it is not too far away she walks. The shopkeeper known as Bees' Knees is a helpful lady and she gives a hand filling up her shopping bags.

The local children love to watch Molly, on her way home from the shop, laden with bags of groceries, four or five bags in her left hand and about the same in her right hand as she waddles along.

As she is plump, short and close to the ground, the bags would not have far to fall, should there be a mishap.

Pokerface Carney could not let such a spectacle pass without comment. He said that Molly is like the Queen Mary making her way into port, all flags flying, but she looks like as if she could go aground before landing.

The kids also love her hat as she always wears a hat when going to the shop. It is best described as floral, multi-coloured and circular which makes a big impression. Nancy Flatfoot says, when she sees her, she says *Look out, the flower garden is approaching.* To be honest, It is quite elegant, very large with a wide prominent rim. Jumbo Jameson remarked that one could park cars on it.

The cuisine is also handled by Molly and the dishes are what both herself and the two sisters fancy. Mind you, their tastes can vary from those of most other people but some may be happy enough with their favourites.

A few examples may help the reader, in this respect. Their dishes include crubeens, spare ribs, rabbit, hare soup, pheasant, perch and frogs legs. It must be said that the triplets look quite healthy on this kind of fare.

Danny the Dope, next door, is into hunting and shooting and he supplies Molly with wildlife such as rabbits, hares and pheasants and the good bit is that they are all free gratis and for nothing. That is what Molly likes best of all. It suits her budget.

Between me and you, I think Danny likes her and maybe, yet, some day, romance might blossom, like a garden in Springtime, but in this case, it could be more like Autumn.

I must now tell you something about Polly and her role in the homestead. Her portfolio includes fashion, footwear, hair and cosmetics. Molly gives her some money and she goes off to the nearest town to make purchases, equipped with sizes, styles and a list of requirements. As she is a bit backward, she allows the staff in the shops to make the choices, in the case of coats, suits, dresses and footwear.

She managed to please the sisters, most times but now and again there were grumbles about colours or quality. Polly herself had a poor dress sense and was usually untidy and scattered.

Polly was the resident hairdresser but as Lily Popcorn said, you would want to have a comprehensive insurance policy before you would let Polly near your hair with a scissors. She's a great chopper, to be sure.

Polly is very much at sea when it comes to cosmetics or makeup. In order to get around this problem she buys a half ton of stuff in the hope that she will have something to please the sisters' tastes.

Recently, when she got home and unwrapped the items, the sisters wanted to know was she about to get them ready to be clowns in the circus. Polly just giggled and sat down at the fire.

Molly gathered up the purchases and threw them into the garbage bin. Then she told Polly that she was cutting her budget for being so stupid, buying rubbish.

I must now say "Hello" to Dolly, the third member of the triplets or as Alfie Fat-Face calls them –"The Blessed Trinity". Dolly has her own special roles to fulfil. She is responsible for public relations, activities and news.

It must be said that she has a very good relationship with the locals as she is well liked by all. For this reason, she has no difficulty getting the latest news to take home to her sisters.

Dolly is good-looking, very tall and slim. Liz Blackberry said the only thing out of joint with her is her neck. It is so long that she could look over Croagh Patrick. That said, she has a nice red face, bright and pleasant, like the morning sun rising.

The past year has been very dramatic in the village of Lusheen and the following is the latest news report supplied by Dolly to her sisters -

Jack the Scratcher was in town all day in Christy the Pig's pub, refuelling and on the way home, his head not being too steady, his High Nellie veered off the road, went careering down the side of a deep quarry, filled with water, submerging the Scratcher. Luckily, he managed to crawl out of the water. A farmer who was tending sheep nearby saw him and helped him back up on to the road. He brought him to his house and offered him a cup of tea, but Scratcher said that he would prefer a whiskey.

The farmer refused the request as he already had more than enough of that. In due course, Scratcher sobered up and was able to continue his journey, on foot, walking with his High Nellie.

Rocker Flanagan is in hospital. He had an altercation with Spout Drudy and he came off second best. His jaw is broken in two places and one of his knees is crushed. He is lucky to be alive. Spout is vicious and very dangerous when ruffled in any way.

Madge Daly is on the drink again. She has lost her head altogether this time. She spends her time now out on the side of the road waving to passers-by and singing *She is far from the land.* When she stops singing she takes a slug out of a bottle and shouts *Wheel out the barrel, we're not in any hurry.*

The night of the bad storm caused huge damage down in the village of Trampstown. It uprooted big trees, blew hay-sheds away like pieces of paper and blew tractors into the local river Daffey. Smiler Thornbird's hat was swept away and he landed himself on top of a heap of farmyard manure. Now he is referred to as Smelly Smiler.

Johnny Jellyfish Jones who lives up in Killskulls had a weird experience last week. You know him. He's a very, very small, little man. As Grinder Duff said about him – *"He's so small, you could blow him off the palm of your hand with your breath".*

Well, he was coming home very late at night last week walking along on a very isolated road. He had been card-playing in Grabber Murtagh's cottage. As he was walking along, he thought he saw lights ahead of him, red lights. As he came nearer, he could see something like a big wall across the road in front of him. He began to get scared and sweat came rolling down his face.

When he came to within yards of the wall he saw a tall figure, in white, beside it. He was skeleton-like and his face was wrinkled. He spoke to Johnny and said – *"I am the ghost of Gorewood Castle, out for the night. I am waiting for my friends, the ghosts of Cloverhill Manor. We are doing one of our haunting sessions".*

Little Johnny was about to collapse when the ghost said – *"Do you want to join me and my friends on our trip or would you prefer to carry on home"?*

Johnny picked up a bit of courage because of the optional offer and he said – *"I would like to go home to bed".* With that, the red lights went dead. The wall moved away and the ghost was gone. Johnny pulled himself together and began to walk as fast as he could until he came near houses with lights on. He was relieved that he had survived.

The following day, the entire area around had the news of Johnny's experience. Some were sceptical and did not believe the story. Others said that it could all be real as they had heard from the old people that the castle and manor mentioned by the ghost were haunted.

The local wise man with the big brain was called in to give a verdict. He was none other than the Ram Rafferty. He claims to be a psycho – therapist. He concluded that Johnny was telling the truth. He was sound of mind, was wide awake and he did not put any drink to his lips because he does not drink. He never walks in his sleep, day or night. He has perfect eyesight. Beyond doubt, Johnny Jellyfish was confronted by a ghost and it was good that his friends did not show up before Johnny walked free.

One thing is certain, he will not be out late at night again, on a lonely road, if he can discipline himself.

As you can see, Dolly does a good job of getting the latest news to her sisters and it is amazing how, even in a small village there can be some dramatic happenings, but then they say, variety is the spice of life.

If you ever happen to be passing through Lusheen, keep an eye out for the blessed three and meeting, even one of them, could make your day. Happy travels!

A word of warning! If you are lucky enough to meet any of the three ladies, please note that as each one has a different portfolio, the one you may meet will only deal with her own Department. As a result, you may be disappointed, if you are looking for answers to some of your questions. For this reason, it may be best to bypass Lusheen.

Christmas Activities in Killnacarn

Christmas was always a special time of year in olden times in Killnacarn which is a small village spread out along the slopes of Bodach Hill. All the houses are thatched cottages. At the west end of it is the cottage of the Dumpling family consisting of Marty, Dolores and eight youngsters.

The four youngest write to *Santa Claus,* some weeks in advance, telling the Red Man what they want for Christmas. Their lists of demands are usually long but Mum edits them and cuts them down to a much shorter form as there is not a barrel of money on tap.

These younger kids also put up the decorations, most of which are home-made by themselves as they are very resourceful. They also make up their own Crib and procure a Christmas tree from their own plantation of trees. They have been trained to be thrifty.

They enjoy putting lighted candles in all the windows for the entire twelve days of Christmas to indicate that their little house is open to welcome the Holy Family.

When it comes to providing the food for the Christmas dinner, their small farm caters for that, also. They have their own potatoes, vegetables and especially the turkey and sometimes they opt for a goose.

Mum, with the help of the older family members, bake bread, a good

Christmas cake and plum pudding.

The one chore they do not perform is the plucking of the turkey. It is done by Squint Mongan who is a very funny man, so he keeps the kids amused.

On Christmas Eve they enjoy going to their little church beside a small wood for midnight Mass. It is magical when there is snow all around, especially on the trees.

The local priest, Fr. Mattie Blackthorn is a very good storyteller and he transports the congregation to Bethlehem and tells the story of the first Christmas – Mary, Joseph and the Child in the manger, the Shepherds, the Magi with their camels and the Star.

On their return from the Church, the kids have refreshments and retire early full of excitement, awaiting the arrival of the man with the beard but before they do so, they have a visit every year from their neighbour, Miss Gwendoline Allsorts.

She is hilarious in her colourful outfit and her capers. She is always in festive mood and well intoxicated. She tells the kids that she is just after having tea with Santa and that he will be dropping in with goodies. She then sings for them – *Santa Claus is Coming to Town.*

They also leave out goodies for Santa, usually, carrots, scones and a glass of milk. When this necessary chore has been executed, they hit for Blanket Street.

They rise while it is still dark and there is a mighty dash to the kitchen to see if Santa has come. They can be worried because Auntie Penelope tells them that Santa gets broken down, on his way, if the weather is bad. She said one year his reindeers refused to work and just lay down in the snow.

They are usually in luck because Santa comes and they are happy enough with what he leaves them.

Sometimes, overnight, there can be a big fall of snow, so they run outside and make a great big snowman and then a snowwoman as well. They pelt snowballs at one another and get drenched.

After that drama, they enjoy their Christmas dinner, sing carols and play games of their own invention as well as making use of some of Santa's edibles.

What makes their Christmas special every year is the custom the family has of giving dinner to a homeless family, a mum a dad and a child. They think of the first Christmas when Mary, Joseph and their baby had no place to stay and ended up in a stable with the animals.

St. Stephen's Day is another bonus occasion for the children because they go hunting the Wren, all disguised with their false faces and outfits. The real perk is that they return home, after visiting numerous houses, with a hat-full of money.

Christmas in Killnacarn is always special but modest, without undue extravagance and the family in question certainly has their priorities right. Moderation in all things is a good approach to living sensibly.

May you too, have a happy Christmas, when it comes around, and maybe you, too, might give a thought and a bit of hospitality to those who may be homeless, hungry and unloved, should any of them knock on your door.

Christmas Day c.1900 © NLI Collection

The Bonfire Tradition in Rosnarolla

I did a very long journey recently to a village noted for many years as a place where old traditions have been preserved, protected and respected. It is called Rosnarolla. This is rare enough, nowadays, as people have moved on to newer things, not that they may be good replacements for the old.

The reason for my journey was to talk to a couple of people who could fill me in on, perhaps, one or two of their traditions. I met a local farmer who was putting his cows into a field and he directed me to the home of Alo Garlic McBride and his wife, Sally Daffodil Macaroni. She always uses her maiden name.

They were not at home when I called but a young lad who was passing by on the road told me that they were down in the paper shop, so, off I went and found them reading a magazine. As soon as I told them what the purpose of my mission was, they were more than willing to help me. You could not meet nicer people, so I was impressed.

We walked back up to their residence and the talking really began then. Sally began by telling me about Bonfire Night which was always the night of the 23rd of June, the Eve of the feast of St. John the Baptist. She told me that the whole idea of the bonfire was to herald the feast on the following day and to draw people's attention to it.

The bonfire was always very popular with the children and young adults because it was an excuse for celebration. The adult population supported the idea also.

For some days prior to the night, there was great bonfire activity, gathering up firewood, turf and any material that was likely to light and burn well. When collected, it all would make a great big pile.

Many fires were located at crossroads or at the head of other roads, for ease of access, but some were lighted on high ground such as on hill slopes or hilltops. The reason for this was, so that the fires could be seen, miles away, as the flames rose upwards in the dark night.

It must be said that the local people usually came out to where the fire was and either sat nearby or stood around, chatting, telling stories, and discussing the latest news. There was often laughter and good cheer. The kids loved to run around the fire, hopping, jumping and singing songs.

Local musicians might arrive and play violins, accordions, flutes and other instruments, adding further to the enjoyment of this outdoor jamboree. The fresh night air was an added bonus.

There could be unwanted happenings at the bonfires, now and again. Sally mentioned a year that a very young boy who was intrigued by the fire, tripped and fell into the flames and got badly burned. He was in hospital for several months.

Another year, a little girl wandered off, in the darkness and a big search was launched. After about two hours they found her, alive and well but bawling crying. She got lost in a huge area of gorse and could not find her way out of it. She said that the parents were greatly relieved.

Sally said that, at the end of the night's celebration they had a custom whereby burning pieces of fuel were taken from the fire and brought to the neighbouring tillage fields and meadows and thrown into them. It was believed that this gesture would bring good luck and ensure that the crops would yield good results.

She ended her recollections by saying that, on the way home from the fire, one could hear the sounds of the wild birds, especially in the bog-lands and the corncrake with his or her very distinctive calling, coming from the meadows.

Sadly, like so many other old traditions, this one has tended to die out also, in recent times, apart from a small number of people who still respect tradition.

It is time now to hear a few words from Alo, a learned man, I am told. He began by saying that it is unlikely that the people attending the bonfires, young or old, would have much knowledge of the saint whose feast they were heralding.

He told me that John the Baptist was six months older than Jesus. His parents were Zechariah and Elizabeth. They lived in Ein Karem, a short distance from Jerusalem. It was there that the Virgin Mary visited her cousin, Elizabeth and there, too, John the Baptist was born.

When John grew up, he had a special mission, to proclaim Jesus as the Lamb of God, to point Him out to the people, the long expected Saviour. He was the one who came before the Lord, to prepare the way before Him. That is why he is called the Precursor, Forerunner or John the Baptiser, even a prophet in Islam. As you may know, he baptised Jesus in the river Jordan.

John the Baptist was a Jew, of course, a wandering or itinerant preacher who preached repentance and forgiveness for sin.

He lived a very austere, penitential and simple life, close to nature and the environment from which he obtained his simple, basic food such as seeds, berries and wild honey.

He dressed like a monk, in a long habit and he wore sandals. Images of him show him holding a lamb.

Herodias, whose first husband was Philip, divorced him and married his brother, Herod Antipas. John objected to the marriage, so she was displeased and was jealous of the Baptist so she devised a plan to kill him. She got her daughter, Salome, to dance for the king and he was so pleased with the dance that he said she could have anything she wished. At her mother's request, she asked for the head of the Baptist and it was delivered to her on a platter.

The Baptist was beheaded at the palace-fortress of Machaerus, near the Dead Sea in Jordan. It was there that Herod's son, Herod Antipas and Herodias lived.

It is said that the Baptist is buried in the Umayyad Mosque in Damascus, Syria.

I thanked both Sally and Alo for their wealth of knowledge and promised them that I would return another day in order to learn more.

Lightning Source UK Ltd.
Milton Keynes UK
UKHW031944170821
388989UK00005B/187